# She's Not You

# She's Not You

## MIMI BARBOUR

SARNA PUBLISHING

This is a work of fiction. Names, characters,

places, and incidents are either the product of the

author's imagination or are used fictitiously,

and any resemblance to actual persons living or dead,

business establishments, events, or locales,

is entirely coincidental.

She's Not You

The Elvis Series – Book 1

Contact Information: mimibarbour66@gmail.com

# Dedication:

This first book of the Elvis Collection is dedicated
to my childhood
heartthrob who I'll never forget or replace,
**Elvis Presley.**
From the time I first started dreaming of sweet
romance, you were my hero. For the many hours of
incredible listening pleasure, I sincerely—and with
love—thank you. Because your songs resonated
with me (the stories hidden in those blues and the
emotion you brought to the words) I've decided that
I wanted to bring some of those very songs to life.
And so the series begins...

# Also Author of...

~*~*~*~

The Vicarage Bench Series
— Spirit Travel at its Best! —
She's Me (Book 1)
He's Her (Book 2)
We're One (Book 3)
Vicarage Bench Anthology (Book 4 – Books 1-3)
Together Again (Book 5)
Together for Christmas (Book 6)
Together Always (Book 7)
***

Angels with Attitude Series
— Angels Playing Cupid! —
The Angels with Attitudes Anthology (Books 1-3)
My Cheeky Angel (Book 1)
His Devious Angel (Book 2)
Loveable Christmas Angel (Book 3)
A Wonderful Life (Book 4)
Mischievous Christmas Angel (Book 5)
***

Elvis Series
— Make an Elvis Song a Book! —
She's Not You (Book 1)
Love Me Tender (Book 2)
Don't Be Cruel ( Book 3 )
***

Vegas Series
— Action–Packed Thrillers! —
Vegas Series – Complete Boxed Set
Partners (Book 1)
Roll the Dice (Book 2)
Vegas Shuffle (Book 3)
High Stakes Gamble (Book 4)
Spin the Wheel (Book 5)
Let it Ride (Book 6)
***

Undercover FBI Series
— Popular & Compelling! —
Special Agent Francesca (Book 1)
Special Agent Finnegan (Book 2)
Special Agent Maximilian (Book 3)
Special Agent Kandice (Book 4)
Special Agent Booker (Book 5)
Special Agent Charli (Book 6)
Special Agent Rylee (Book 7)
Special Agent Murphy (Book 8)
Special Agent Sophia (Book 9)

Special Agent Hunter (Book 10)
Special Agent Makayla (Book 11 – to be released
spring of 2021)
***
Holiday Heartwarmers Series
— Truly a Christmas favorite! —
Holiday Heartwarmers Trilogy
Please Keep Me (Book 1)
Snow Pup (Book 2)
Find Me a Home (Book 3)
Frosty the Snowman (Book 4)
Love of my Life (Book 5)
A Perfect Storm (Book 6)
Alone at Christmas (Book 7)
***
Her Sweet Revenge Series
— She's unstoppable! —
Retaliation (Book #1) FREE
Justice (Book #2)
Resolution (Book #3
Endings – (Book #4)
Faith (Book #5)
Leni (Book #6)
~*~*~
Single Title Series
He's My Baby (Book #1)
Christmas Runaway (Book #2)

Because You Cared (Book #3)
Daddy's Mine (Book #4)
Her Hero (Book #5 )
You Make Me Happy (Book #6)
Sweet Christmas (Book #7)
You're the Boss (Book 8)

\*\*\*

The Best in Romance Series
Red Hot Divas (Book #1 Box Set)
Hot and Handsome (Book #2 Box Set

~\*~\*~\*~

Other Titles
I'm No Angel
Hotshot Cowboy
Big Girls Don't Cry
The Surrogate's Secret
Mimi's Mix (Box Set)
'Tis the Season (Box Set)
Hearts, Flowers & Romance (Box Set)
Love, Christmas (Multi-author Box Set)
Unforgettable Romances (Multi-author Box Set)
Sweet and Sassy (Multi-author Box Set)
Unforgettable Heroes (Multi-author Box Set)
Unforgettable Christmas (Multi-author Box Set)
A Christmas She'll Remember (Multi-author Box Set)
Unforgettable Valentine (Multi-author Box Set)

A Valentine She'll Remember (Multi-author Box Set)
Unforgettable Suspense (Multi-author Box Set)
Unforgettable Danger (Multi-author Box Set)
Unforgettable Trouble (Multi-author Box Set)
Unforgettable Weddings (Multi-author Box Set)
A Wedding She'll Remember (Multi-author Box Set)
Sweet and Sassy Brides (Multi-author Box Set)
Love, Christmas 2 (Multi-author Box Set)
Sweet and Sassy Suspense (Multi-author Box Set)
Unforgettable Thrills (Multi-author Box Set)
Unforgettable Passion (Multi-author Box Set)
A Romance She'll Remember (Multi-author Box Set)
Sweet and Sassy Cinderella (Multi-author Box Set)
Unforgettable Power (Multi-author Box Set)
Daring Protectors (Multi-author Box Set)
Unforgettable Charmers (Multi-author Box Set)
Sweet and Sassy Baby Love (Multi-author Box Set)
Sweet and Sassy Heroes (Multi-author Box Set)
Unforgettable Intrigue (Multi-author Box Set)
Unforgettable Christmas Dreams (Multi-author Box Set)

Sweet and Sassy Holiday (Multi-author Box Set)
Christmas Shorts (Multi-author Box Set)
Unforgettable Temptations (Multi-author Box Set)
Unforgettable Surrender (Multi-author Box Set)
Unforgettable Deceptions (Multi-author Box Set)
Unforgettable Joy (Multi-author Box Set)
Unforgettable Sweethearts (Multi-author Box Set)
Unforgettable Christmas Joy (Multi-author Box Set)
Dear Santa – A Christmas Wish (Multi-author Box Set)
New Year's Eve Shorts (Multi-author Box Set)
Unforgettable Revenge (Multi-author Box Set )
Thrilling Suspenseful Nights (A Fabulous Freebie Set)

\*\*\*

All Mimi's books can be found on her Amazon Author Page:
http://bit.ly/MimiBarbourAmazon
OR
Website: http://mimibarbour.com

# Praise for She's Not You:

"Mimi introduces a lady in distress and a bachelor who can't cook. Then she adds an adorable little girl who knows how to get her way, a dysfunctional brother-in-law, and an oversized puppy. Here's a Christmas story to warm anyone's heart."

*~reviewed by Best-selling author, Nancy Radke*

"Another adorable romance from Mimi Barbour. I love Christmas books with cute children and pets, so this immediately caught my attention. A kind-hearted hero who rescues a woman in distress is always a winner with me. Drama, romance and Christmas spirit fill this book, which is just right for this time of year."

*~reviewed by Loves Reading*

"Such a heartwarming book loved this book very much would recommend this book to anyone. It is

what romance is about."
*~reviewed by Kindle customer*

# Chapter 1

Jesse Parker stepped out of the apartment's elevator into the dimly lit corridor where the wall light flickered, warning all of its impending demise. He stopped dead. She was there again, the little girl who tore at his heartstrings.

Same as she'd done the last couple of days, as soon as the pixie-like child saw him, she wiped her wet face, jumped up from where she huddled on the hallway's green carpet, and beelined for her apartment door. Only, this time she hesitated before she opened it. Her little back faced him, a wall of antagonism shielding her body slapped at Jesse until he felt his insides sinking.

Why he frightened her, he didn't know. So he waited, not wanting to make things worse. Speaking as softly as a deep male voice can, he said, "Is there something I can help you with, sweetie?"

He'd seen her tears. In fact, he'd seen them every time she'd run away. And they drove him crazy.

"My mommy's sick." The tear-streaked side of her still baby-faced cheeks was all she showed him. Somewhere between the ages of four to six, he thought—until she spoke and then he wondered if she were even younger.

What the heck did he know about kids? Standing there, trying not to frighten the little cherub, plans scuttled through his head like mice at the smell of a cat.

Instincts kicked in and he crouched down to her level. "Has she seen the doctor?"

"Uh huh! He's dumb." The child used her arm to wipe the mess off her face and a small sob escaped. "All he tells her is to take pills but she mostly bawfs them up. She bawfs a lot." Before Jesse could say anything else, the tiny sprite opened her door and disappeared.

*Now, what the hell am I supposed to do?* Jesse knew he couldn't leave it alone. He stood with his hand raised to knock and then slowly lowered it when a sudden thought changed his mind.

He'd try to contact his sister, Kim. After all, it was her apartment he was staying in, and knowing how gregarious she was, Jesse had no doubt that she most likely knew these neighbors and could tell him something about their situation.

The thought of doing nothing had disappeared

the moment he'd picked up the scent of the child's fear and heard her husky, frightened voice.

A short way down the hall, Jesse stormed into his sister's apartment, closed the door, and caught his breath. He'd forgotten how she'd rigged the switch to turn on all the holiday decorations she'd set up around the place.

Her oversized Christmas tree sat in front of the main set of windows in the large room and blazed its magic at him, flashing twice. The windows behind did a great job of reflecting the splendor. The hundreds, or most likely thousands, of lights twinkled from both inside the branches and around the outer edges.

The theme of the tree had to be angels or maybe fairies since Kim had hundreds of tiny feathered creatures in all colors poking out from every space. Then there were ribbons inter-woven between these sprites gleaming with the sparkling surfaces of silver and pearl.

*Bah!* The girl might be his sister but she was a nutcase when it came to this season. Mind you, he had to admit that Christmas made Kim a living. A very good one if her place was anything to go by. A few years back when he'd first seen her home, he'd been appalled. With Jesse's help, now the condo she owned was not only modern but very comfortable.

The sound of claws scraping the floor for leverage warned him that Sam had heard him enter. A chubby canine with bright black eyes and flopping ears hurled itself straight for him, expecting he'd break the momentum of this unrestrained dash.

This time it didn't work. Unprepared, Jesse couldn't catch Sam and he tumbled ass over teakettle up against the wall. Obviously unhurt, the silly dog stood up with a wobble or two and then made a second attempt.

Quickly, Jesse removed his jacket, scooped up the frenzied pup, and sat in the only chair in the place that would accommodate his size comfortably.

Once he'd settled the four-legged pest to chewing on the small rawhide bone he carried around in his pocket, Jesse dialed Kim's cell number and she answered at once.

"Kim, it's me. I've just had an encounter with this kid in the hallway for the third day in a row and each time she sees me she runs away. Today she was bawling and said her mommy is sick. Do you know these people two doors down from you?"

"Oh no! Belle must be getting worse. I guess Yaya is fretting. She gets scared, poor little tyke. Usually, she comes to get me. But she knows I'm away. Jesse, you've got to do something."

"Hey, brat. You've got me here looking after your

herd, keeping your plants and now you want me to babysit your sick neighbor. Sorry, I draw the line at barfing mommies. She must have *someone* I can call to help her."

Kim laughed at his grumpiness as he knew she would. She never took him seriously, probably because he frequently wasn't. "Come on, there are only two cats and one little puppy, and admit it—they're all beautiful. To answer your other question, no. Belle hasn't anyone to help. Yaya's father is dead, killed in Iraq, and as far as I know, the girls are on their own. I help out when I can."

To cover up the ping his soft heart just delivered, he asked, "Yaya? What kind of crazy name is that?" He scoffed, couldn't help it.

Kim laughed again. "Her real name is Layla but she couldn't pronounce it when she was younger and called herself Yaya. It stuck. Belle adores her baby, so it must be difficult for her to see Yaya so scared."

"Does she have a doctor or a boss, someone to help her?"

"Belle had to take a medical leave from her job at the playschool where she worked. The pain in her stomach gets so severe that she's bent over a lot of the time. Plus, she says she lives in a fog and can't seem to concentrate. Being a war widow, her medical coverage helps some but there are still certain procedures they've refused to pay for and she can't personally afford the costs for these tests. I know she's terrified it might be cancer and that scares me too. It's a real tangle, Jesse. I feel so helpless most of the time. I know you'll help though and it makes me less worried." Her theatrical sigh, heavy and heartfelt, wrenched at his strength of will.

Okay, now that's what got to him. His sister figured Jesse was one step down from God; that he could do anything. Most of the time he tried to disabuse her of this idea but she wouldn't accept the truth. So Jesse invariably found himself trying to live up to her expectations.

You'd think after all these years of jumping to do her bidding, he'd be able to let the hero status go, make her wake up and see the real world. He just couldn't. She'd look at him with those big green eyes so very like the mother he'd adored, and poof, there went his resolutions.

Weakness sifted into his attitude and he felt the moment his backbone dissolved, and he flipped to his role of being her big, weak-kneed, fix-it brother. As her voice coerced, softness filtered through his determination.

"Damn, Kim! What do you expect me to do? I don't even know the woman and Layla runs from me every time we meet." Not quite the truth, but his nosy sibling didn't have to know about their latest encounter.

Jesse had learned his lesson a long time ago to keep certain personal information from Kim who dedicated herself to trying to bring him happiness in the form of a wife.

After the last debacle, she'd backed off, swearing she had no idea that the girl she'd forced him to date had been a recovering drug addict who hadn't quite recovered... as he'd soon found out when he'd had to rescue her from a ladies' room of the restaurant where she'd gotten into some bad stuff and needed an ambulance. Talk about a mess! The night in the emergency ward hadn't helped his temper. When Kim had called the next morning anxious to see if her matchmaking had worked, for the first time she'd suffered his wrath.

He'd hung up on her and she'd done everything she could to wiggle her way back into his good graces. Since then, she'd stayed out of his personal life and left well-enough alone. Until now.

Out of the blue, she'd come begging, wanting him to stay at her condo for the holidays. Because one of her three stores had a huge problem, Jesse was needed. She'd pleaded in the exact way she'd done as a girl growing up under the protection of a doting brother.

The manager she'd installed in her Christmas store in Olympia had been in a car accident and would be hospitalized for at least a month. Since the shop had just opened that summer, there was no one trained yet to take over responsibility.

Seeing that December brought in huge profits in her business, Kim couldn't afford to let just anyone step into the spot. She'd have to go herself. And that meant leaving her place in a huge hurry, along with her two furry white Persians, one very spoiled golden Lab named Sam—a puppy who thought himself a warrior—and a bowl full of exotic fish.

She needed an all-purpose petsitter. At Christmas, all her many friends had plans. Lucky for her she had a soft-hearted, soft-headed brother.

Jesse couldn't claim work as an excuse because Kim knew he'd just put the For Sale sign up on the latest house he'd built. Therefore, he had a break until he found the next property to buy in the coming year. Guess the week of skiing he'd planned in Aspen took second place to a little sister with a shattered voice full of tears.

Before he could stop her flow of words, a loud pounding on the door got his attention. "Someone's at the door, Sis. I'll call back later."

Jesse hung up. Then made his way over and

opened the door. A tiny tornado flew past him screaming. "Kimmy, you gotta come. Mommy's dead!"

# Chapter 2

Jesse felt as if he'd been shot. A crying three-year-old was one thing. A dead woman was completely not acceptable. What the hell was he to do?

He watched the screamer run frantically from the entrance of one room to the other, calling for Kimmy with a hysterical puppy jumping up and down alongside.

The only way he could stop the child was by swinging her up into his arms. Not knowing what to expect, when her arms wrapped a chokehold around his throat, it utterly destroyed him.

She buried her wet face into his neck and hiccupped her words, "I want *Kimmy*."

"Sweetheart, Kim's away for a few days. I'm Jesse, her big brother. Now, tell me what's happened." He kept his voice soft yet firm. While he talked, he carried her toward the apartment she'd just left.

"Mommy fell down and won't move." Anxious eyes, globby with tears, wrenched at his heart.

Green! They were the same green as Kim's babied Persian cats. Deep, dark irises surrounded by velvet.

Jesse's heart thudded into higher gear without him being able to do a thing to stop it from happening. His arms tightened instinctively around the small body as if to protect her from any horrors awaiting them. Once they arrived, he lowered her onto a chair nearby and patted her head. "Stay here while I help your mom."

Then he ran to the woman's body on the floor.

Reaching toward her neck, he jumped when she groaned and moved. Thank the good Lord! The woman was alive.

Yaya, who'd left the chair the moment she'd seen her mommy shift, struggled past his reaching arms, flew around to the other side and faced her mom. Her little hand gently gathered the sweat-coated blonde locks and pushed them away from the thin face of the young woman trying desperately to rouse.

Not stopping to think about the right or wrong of the situation, Jesse gathered the slight woman in his arms, lifting the lightweight as if he carried a fragile parcel too precious to be manhandled.

In the meantime, Yaya pulled back the cover on the sofa and waited for Jesse to lay her mother down. Then the precocious sweetheart covered her groaning mother, tucking the hand-made afghan around her body.

Her tiny hand reached to pat her cheek and Jesse watched as the woman took the hand and gave it a kiss.

Her voice throaty and wobbling, she said, "Mama's okay now, Layla. I'm sorry I scared you, honey. I shouldn't have tried to stand up when I was so dizzy. I guess I fainted." She pushed the wildly unkempt hair from her daughter's face. "Who's your friend?"

Layla crawled up beside her mother on the sofa and cuddled. She sniffed and said, her little-girl's voice heartbreaking, "Jesse's weally not a stranger, Mommy. He's Kimmy's brother."

Jessie watched the byplay, amusement filling up space where fright had resided only moments earlier.

He braced himself to be interrogated, but he didn't ready himself for the effect of the biggest, cat-like eyes of soft emeralds highlighted by diamonds he'd ever seen—like mother, like daughter. The surrounding face appeared colorless which, no doubt, greatly enhanced the beauties under her thick lashes. The woman's feverish appearance worried him, which had him reaching for his cellphone.

"What are you doing?"

"I'm calling for an ambulance."

"Don't! Stop!" Her arm reached his way and her hand waved at him.

So, she wasn't that far gone. He lifted his finger before pressing send. "No choice. You were passed out. I'm not a doctor but it doesn't take a rocket scientist to know you need one."

"I went to my doctor this morning. He's an idiot with a diagnosis that's ridiculous." She spit the words toward him while struggling to sit upright and not disturb Layla.

Impressed with the kind way she behaved toward her daughter, he watched her caring maneuvers until her assertive nature flashed annoyance in his direction, then he began to fear for his safety. Jesse's hands lifted automatically with his palms facing her. He stepped back once and then again, careful to get out of the path of her raising ire.

Shoulder-length blonde hair, caught under her chin and spread over her shoulders, looked neglected and not at all attractive. In fact, nothing about this skinny broad looked appetizing to Jesse other than her eyes.

A voice inside nudged him to leave, get out while he still had the chance. Paying attention to the familiar warning, as he'd done since a young fellow, he put the phone away. "If you don't like this guy, go to another doctor." *Damn, he just couldn't keep his mouth shut!* His feet took over and moved him another step back.

"I no longer have health insurance. I take what I can get at the closest free clinic and that leaves me stuck with the pathetic numbskull who swore I had Irritable Bowel Syndrome because he hasn't a clue to what my problem really is. Look, it's obvious you want to leave. Go! We're fine now. I haven't been able to eat anything, so I feel weaker than usual. If I rest for a few minutes, I'll be fine."

Layla sat up and looked at Jesse, fear written over her face as plain as if she'd screamed the words *'Don't leave me!'*

The little darling, whose pants looked to be on backward and whose t-shirt had stains of milk mixed with peanut butter, left her mother's side and stepped toward him. She took his hand, moving slowly in case he scared her.

*Caught!* He was sinking and he knew it. While annoyance blistered his insides, he didn't have the skill to cover it up. The woman saw his struggle and the cocky grin she shared with him didn't quite make up for his frustration. She'd most likely been at the mercy of these eyes a time or two herself.

Stiffening his determination to not get involved, he crouched down and waited, not wanting to send Layla scuttling for cover.

The girl's blonde hair, white gold, stuck out all her over her head in thick straight spikes, looking as if a lawnmower had gone berserk. Her timidity seemed faked and for a few seconds, he wondered if he was being played by a genius.

"Will you help us like Auntie Kimmy does? She makes us *supper* when Mommy isn't feeling good."

Jesse looked toward the grinning patient on the couch for help and got back a smirking shrug. Stiffening his spine, he began to shake his head and refuse Layla's plea.

That was when the little darling stepped in-between his opened knees, stared up into his eyes and said the one word designed to crumple his resolve.

"Ple-ease!"

# Chapter 3

Belle watched as Jesse Parker, the handsome brother of her friend from down the hall, tried to hold his own against a master at manipulation. Her Yaya, the little actress, had skills even she hadn't seen yet. Probably came from watching too much of the idiot box on the stand in the corner. Not Belle's first choice, but this ongoing sickness had loosened her restrictions both on herself and Yaya.

Belle saw Jesse look her way, and his confused yet gentle gray eyes almost proved to be her downfall. Almost.

Kim tended to brag about her brother, a lot. In truth, she'd started to promote him like a hot movie or a best-selling novel and this type of behavior turned Belle right off. She'd gotten so fed up with the blah, blah that she'd hoped never to have to meet the guy who was perfection in jeans according to his enamored sibling. Belle didn't believe anyone could live up to that kind of hype. Now she wasn't so sure.

The dude was priceless in his interaction with Yaya.

Jesse's look begged for help. Bored, and needing some form of entertainment, Belle kind of wanted him to stick around as much as her little princess. Being picked up in his strong arms as if she weighed nothing, which unfortunately was the case, had her libido sending out hot little signals.

Scared he'd read her response in her reddened face, Belle looked at her dry, chapped hands and then hid them. Under her breath, she grumbled a favorite phrase, one she'd learned from her English father as a teenager. "Bloody hell!" Why did she have to look her worst and feel the same?

Her grumbling comment snared Jesse's attention for only a few seconds. Then he turned back to the matter at hand, trying to make Yaya understand his predicament. "Look sunshine, I'm not like my sister. I'm a rotten cook."

Just as Belle knew would happen, Yaya had the perfect solution. "That's okay. We could order pizza."

*Bingo!* Her baby loved pizza. Feeling sorry for Jesse, Belle broke into their conversation. "Hold it, Yaya. You can't force Mr. Parker to take pity on us and arrange dinner. I'll make something in a little while."

With his eyebrow raised and his head cocked, Jesse turned her way, questioning her sanity. Then he spoke. "You're definitely not up to cooking tonight, Miss... ahhh, Belle. I'll order some pizza like Layla suggested, and we can share." His shrug spoke to her and made her grin. If shoulders could talk, his were saying, *"what the hell! It's just for a little while and then I'm outta here."*

Before she could argue, Layla, the little monkey, danced her glee jig and clapped her hands. "We're having pizza. Yay!"

Belle sifted her fingers through her mop of loose hair and flipped it to the side. She had no money to pay for the pizza Yaya now had her heart set on. "That's really nice of you, Jesse, but it's out of our budget."

"My treat," he said, in a nice way, obviously not wanting to embarrass her any further.

Belle realized that Yaya had stopped talking and was physically holding her breath. How could she disappoint since her baby hardly ever got treats anymore?

"Then we accept and with pleasure. By the way, my name is Belle Foster and this little monster is Layla, more often known as Yaya."

He looked her way and Belle noticed his perusal of her skinny body in jeans too large and a sweater too big. Damn but this sickness had turned her into a scarecrow, someone she didn't recognize.

She hated that her young life had been reduced to a quagmire of health problems. Apparently, problems with no answers, or at least none she'd found.

Life had been good until one day earlier in the year. She'd noticed certain symptoms had worsened to where she had trouble coping with anything and everything. Her stomach, always a little unsettled, became her worst enemy.

Sick days, never used until this dilemma, had finally run out and she had to give up her job. As much as her boss wanted her to stay, they both agreed that being continuously short-staffed in the daycare hurt the kids and was unfair to the other workers.

Illness not only invaded, it wouldn't let up. Each day it had gotten worse, to where she lived in a constant fog of indecision and fear. What would happen to her baby if she couldn't beat this crisis?

Downsizing to save money, she'd moved into this building, met up with Kim Parker and things had improved slightly.

With Kim around, Belle didn't feel quite so alone in dealing with her difficulties. Her new friend had gotten into the habit of stopping by before breakfast and after work so she could organize meals for her and Layla. On Belle's worst days, she'd even wash their clothes and spend time housecleaning so that the untidiness wasn't as bad.

On the days that Belle felt better, she'd cook meals and bake, then freeze it all to use when she was worse. A vicious circle of bad and not-so-bad had them in its clutches.

Money was tight, and if it weren't for her savings and the help she got from the government, she didn't know what she'd do. Mind you, that wouldn't last forever.

While being coached by the tiny pro-pizza fan, Jesse placed the order for their meal. Yaya, glowing from his unexpected attention, ran to get the dolls she'd coerced Jesse into showing some interest in meeting. While he waited for her to return, he came to perch on the chair kitty-corner to the sofa where Belle spent far too much time.

He spoke low as if afraid that Yaya would hear. "Have you eaten *anything* at all today? You look kinda frail."

"You mean skinny."

"You said it, not me." Again his hands shot up.

She laughed, surprised at how much better the levity made her feel. "I had some crackers earlier. When I get like this, it's all I can eat. But then the pains get worse and my stomach revolts."

Belle had no idea what made her tell him the truth

about her condition. Usually, she made up some fib about the flu and changed the subject. After all, no one liked to hear doom and gloom and health bitches, especially from a twenty-five-year-old.

Before he could answer, Layla re-appeared dragging her chest of baby dolls and the clothes Belle had made for them. While Jesse exclaimed over all the tiny crocheted outfits that Yaya held up for his inspection, Belle reached for the plate of biscuits and started to nibble.

Jesse's hand moved like greased lightning as he stopped her from taking the next bite.

"Are these made with wheat?"

"I think so. They're soda crackers."

"You say that's all you've eaten today?"

"I guess so. Everything else I try seems to upset me. I had toast yesterday and fruit, but it didn't sit well. It's crazy. When I eat very little, it's not so bad. Then, when I get so hungry I'm forced to try something, I choose the blandest stuff I can. No spicy foods, no grease. My stomach is so tender, even fruit and vegetables go right through. It's horrible." Belle's voice broke and she had to stop. His sympathy had undone her like no one else's, and she had the insane notion that if she crawled over on his lap and just snuggled into his arms, she'd be better. Tears sprung, emotions attacked and she had to hide her face. Without thinking, she lifted the cracker to take another bite.

He tackled her hand before it reached her mouth and stopped her. "Don't." His tone caught her attention and she stopped.

"Why not? I certainly can't eat the pizza."

He held her hand gently and his thumb rubbed at the skin. "I have a young fellow who works with me sometimes; he's an apprentice studying for his carpenter's ticket. The guy natters on constantly and most times I shut him off but I remember him telling me about his mom being sick like you. Her symptoms were also food-related. Seems she had a problem with eating things with wheat. Once they put her on a gluten-free diet, she started getting better. He called it Celiac."

"I've heard of it, just never thought it had anything to do with me." Her hand opened and the cracker fell to the floor. Then she entwined her fingers with his. "Oh my God! Could... could it be so simple?"

At her tone, Yaya hopped up from the floor, stopped dressing her baby doll with the little sweater-set she'd promised to show Jesse, and ran to her mom. "What's wrong, Mommy?"

Belle lifted the little doll into her arms and hugged. With all the emotions flooding her system, joy mixed with trepidation and a good healthy fear that it might not be so; she had to hide her excitement.

*Could it really be that simple?*

# Chapter 4

Jesse watched as Belle processed his information. He saw the anxiety that stayed after all the other feelings filtered through her thoughts. A strange urge possessed him that he had to fight against. The urge to take her on his knee, rock her against his body, and whisper encouragement to believe. Sometimes things in life really were that uncomplicated.

The doorbell broke into the moment and Layla struggled out of her mother's clinging arms and ran to his side. She reached for his hand to pull him to his feet. "The pizza man's here, Jesse. We have to pay him and then we can eat. I'm so hungwy! Are you hungwy?"

Jesse grinned with delight. No wonder Kim wanted him to meet this darling. She knew he had a soft spot for angels with golden hair, big green eyes, and a lisp.

After all, she'd been about Layla's age and with

the same precocious nature when she'd discovered that Jesse, five years older than her, couldn't say no to her childish demands. He'd tried, many times, but her talent in using her eyes and her voice in just the perfect way was his downfall.

"Okay, sunshine. Let's go pay the man and we'll have dinner."

A short time later, Layla had her pizza on a plate and was hunkered down on the floor beside her mom.

"Do you want a bite, Mama? It's de-licious! Jesse says I can eat it with my hands. So you *can't* get mad at me. Wight?"

Jesse knew he looked sheepish, tried to wipe the telltale sign off his face, and failed dismally. "Pizza tastes better when you pick it up in your hands. I told her not to touch anything until she wipes away any mess she makes with her napkin."

"It's okay. I used to eat my pizza the same way." Belle smiled at her little girl and ruffled her hair. Then she made as if to rise.

He stopped her. "You need to have something too. We can't sit in front of you and gorge ourselves if you have no food. Look, do you have any eggs? I can make you a fairly plain omelet."

"I do." She swallowed before continuing. "Jesse, I can't thank you enough for being here in this emergency. For giving me hope when I... I had almost given up. You can't know how much I want Celiac to be the answer." Belle continued to sift her fingers through Yaya's hair as her little girl enjoyed her special treat. "Tell the truth, I can't stop thinking of the possibilities, and how it will improve our life."

***

As Belle's savior strode from the room, the sexy, manly sway of his hips caught her attention. Being able to read a person's character, one of her better skills, let her know that he had no idea just how amazingly suggestive his movements were. Or that they might dazzle any red-blooded woman into shuddering reactions and erotic fantasies.

Belle stretched her cramped limbs and knew she should be in the kitchen helping, trying to do something for herself. However, the weakness that had flooded her system and brought on her faint hadn't let up at all. She didn't trust herself not to drop to the floor again. Guess a person can't survive on a few crackers and milk for days on end.

Also, the thought of pulling the same stunt in front of Yaya kept her in a prone position with her legs up. No way she wanted to terrify her child twice in a few hours.

As it was, her Yaya, who had always been a happy

child, showed signs of becoming withdrawn and sad. Belle had even noticed the telltale trace of dried tears on her face when she'd caught her sneaking in from the hallway.

She questioned her and Yaya admitted to waiting for Kim who hadn't been to visit for a number of days. For a three-year-old, explanations of her neighbor's need to transfer to the other store didn't stick. In her mind, because she wanted Kim to appear as she'd always done, it should just happen. No doubt, the poor little doll felt safer with the other woman around and Belle didn't blame her.

The doorbell rang once again and Yaya looked to her for permission to answer the summons. Before she could, Jesse reappeared with a questioning look. Belle nodded and he went to open the door to her caller.

A man in the uniform of the American armed forces waited impatiently. He had a cane in one hand and a bouquet of flowers in the other. As soon as he spied Belle, he burst into the room, limping past Jesse to stop in front of her.

"Belle. Baby. I found you. Warned you I would, didn't I?"

Belle almost slid off the sofa in her anxiety to back away from the man. Unfortunately, his delight at seeing her had dismantled some brain cells because he didn't pick up on her dismay or her immediate withdrawal.

However, Jesse must have. Without hesitation, he grabbed the man from behind to yard him away from the sofa where Belle lay. But things obviously didn't work out the way he'd planned. Belle saw Jesse's surprise when he found himself held up against the wall with Jack's arm across his throat and searing anger staring at him from cold, black eyes. "Back off, asshole."

Belle screamed and fought her way off the couch to grab a frightened Layla in her arms. "Let him go, Jack. I mean it."

Jack looked in her direction and his momentary lack of pressure was enough for Jesse to turn the tables. This time Jesse held the upper hand while Jack's arm was twisted behind his back so high that any movement brought pain. No doubt, Jesse, being the tallest and strongest of the two, wouldn't be caught out again.

He put his face close to Jack's and talked low. "What's your problem, pal? And who the hell are you to bust in here like you own the place?"

"I'm Belle's fiancé, that's who I am. Now let me go. And then leave."

# Chapter 5

Belle was horrified that her husband's brother, Jack, had found them. Besides a lack of funds, he'd been the other reason she'd given up their old apartment.

Now here he was again making trouble for her. Trouble she didn't need in her life at this point. Feeling the way she did was enough burden for anyone to face. Losing a job she loved and worked at so hard because sickness prevented her from carrying out her duties already had her downhearted and depressed.

It seems as if she couldn't run far enough. She'd have to deal with this unruly man whose personal trauma from the conflict in Iraq had dismantled some brain cells.

Her husband, Terry, would be horrified if he knew his well-loved baby brother had sunk to this kind of behavior, manhandling a guest in Belle's home.

Once the tables had turned and Jesse had Jack up against the wall, Belle felt her spirits lift. She had the insane impulse to pump her fist and roll her arm a few times while yelling. "Yesss!"

Yaya sniffled and pressed her head against Belle's stomach, which reminded her that they had to calm the situation not encourage more violence. Jack needed to leave, quietly.

"Let him go, Jesse, please."

He did as she asked, but reluctantly. With eyes watchful, Jesse strode over to where she and Yaya huddled on the sofa. He stood nearby with his arms crossed and a 'don't mess with me' sneer on his face.

Jack straightened his uniform, ran his fingers through the overly-long hair not normally seen on a GI and reached for his cane that had fallen when he'd jumped to the attack. His back stiffened and like magic, he took on the respectful appearance of a soldier, a man of honor. He strode toward Belle and stopped when Jesse moved forward also.

"Belle, honey, is this any way to treat family? I missed you and Layla. It wasn't right for you to take off without letting me know you were moving. No forwarding address or even a goodbye note saying it's been nice to know you."

"I'm sorry, Jack, but you wouldn't stay away from the apartment or my place of work. And your behavior annoyed my boss and was scaring Layla. I couldn't let you ruin our lives that way."

The soldier crumpled, and the traumatized individual appeared. "What about *my* life?" he whined. "Losing Terry almost killed me. Being kept stateside with no deployment in sight has made my life a living hell. Then to top that off, my fiancée leaves me."

"That's just it, Jack. I'm not your fiancée. You won't accept that and we both know I can't marry you."

A feverish excitement filled Jack's face. He dropped to his knees, inched closer to Belle, and grabbed for her hand. In the meantime, Layla scuttled away from her mom and ran straight to Jesse, who picked her up automatically and turned her face away from the spectacle being played out in front of him.

Belle's voice softened with pity and regret. She let him hold her hand. "Jack, I've told you over and over. I loved Terry. But he's gone now. I *don't* love you. It's time for both of us to move on."

The expression in Jack's eyes worried her. There was pain mixed with disbelief and just enough anger brewing to make her very uncomfortable. If she didn't know better, she might be tempted to believe she'd broken his heart. But there was never anything between them. Other than what he'd manufactured in his own imagination.

She tried to extricate her hand from the painful grip Jack now inflicted.

"You don't mean that. Terry and I were twins. I'm his other half. If you cared about him, then you have to love me too. I need you to care. There's no one else."

Conflicts rioted inside of Belle. The churning in her stomach overwhelmed her and if Jack hadn't been in the way, she'd have doubled over.

Staring into the beseeching gaze of a man who wasn't using his meds, a man who'd recently stalked her and frightened her half to death, made her feel like all hope had fled. Her eyes closed and she couldn't fight off the blackness any longer, in fact, she welcomed it.

When she came to, all she saw was Jesse's worried face and an empty room behind him.

She struggled to sit up even as he held her down. "Yaya?"

"She's fine, getting her pajamas on. And Jack's gone. Once you passed out, his mind seemed to wander back to some crazy action he'd witnessed in Iraq and he couldn't get away from here fast enough."

"Thank goodness! He scares me silly, Jesse. The sad part is that he was a wonderful guy before being deployed. My husband, Terry, could be a bit of a jerk when things didn't go his way, but Jack always kept his cool. He was sweet and good-natured, a person who I'd have welcomed into our lives."

Belle pictured Jack as he used to be, always a smile and a kind word. He'd put Terry in his place a few times when he'd turn into a spoiled jackass.

"And now?" Jesse asked, his face watchful.

"The way he is now... well, it terrifies me. I don't want him near me or Yaya. Aggression in any shape isn't acceptable to me, Jesse, and I couldn't have her being intimidated and frightened whenever he'd lose it."

"He's that unpredictable?"

"He is now. At first, when he came back alive, we were ecstatic to see him. Then the PTSD got worse and he'd react in every situation with such negativity and belligerence that he became frightening. You saw him. He'd turn up at our apartment all the time and want me to marry him and take care of him. When that got too much, I tried to put a stop to it. So he changed tactics. Instead of the apartment, he'd show up at the daycare where I worked and frighten the children."

"Was that what made you quit?" Jesse seemed enthralled with her story and she felt at ease enough to continue.

"I didn't quit. My boss let me go—so I would get

social assistance." Her painful truth was out now and if it repulsed him, she'd understand. Feeling like a loser, she expected that everyone else would see her that way also. She was wrong.

"Sometimes a person has to do what she's got to do. You had Layla to look after. Did Jack get you fired?"

"He became part of the reason. Mostly, it was because of the sick days. My boss tried to keep me on for as long as possible but they required an employee who would show up every day, someone healthy enough to keep up with the kids. I'd lost that ability months ago. Hell, I can hardly get out of bed each day to take care of my own baby."

Tears welled and she bit her lip to stop them from falling. Crying and self-pity were not in her nature. She'd always been strong; a stiff-upper-lip kinda girl with a strong determination to overcome any obstacle thrown in her path.

She'd worked her way out of the ghetto where she'd grown up, hating the slums and disliking her folks who'd let life bring them down.

Their screaming arguments had kept her from sleeping many nights, her pillow wrapped around her head to try and keep out the hateful words.

They'd finally split when she'd been an older teenager and both had disappeared from her life.

Her father remarried a woman who had a daughter of her own and he'd moved them to another state.

Her mother joined up with some strange bearded man who'd taken a fancy to her warped sense of humor. They lived in the Yukon.

Feeding her ambitions, Belle had worked two and three jobs to be able to enroll into nursing. Then she'd met Terry and the four years of schooling became two as she downgraded to achieve an associate's degree in early childhood education. They'd needed her wages since his Army pay didn't cover the expenses he'd accumulated from years of overspending.

"Mommy, I bwushed my hair all by myself." Layla ran into the room, her spikes flattened somewhat with water and a heavy hand.

She wore pink pajamas with colorful kitties bouncing everywhere. She'd grown out of them somewhat as perceived by the pants not quite reaching her ankles and the shirt snug across her chest.

Belle noticed that she'd done the buttons up incorrectly but said nothing.

"It looks lovely, babe. You did a wonderful job. You remember your promise, right? No more taking the scissors and giving yourself a haircut. Either I will do it for you or Kim."

"Can Jesse cut my hair?" Layla climbed up on Jesse's lap as if she had all the right in the world and the big guy melted in front of Belle's eyes.

"Did you ask permission to use Jesse for your personal armchair?" Belle returned his smile since he seemed to get a kick out of her question.

"I don't need to, do I?" Yaya turned her big green eyes full-force toward Jesse. She even fluttered her eyelashes like some cheeky lass in a romantic Regency film. All that was missing was a fan.

Jesse laughed and hugged her little body, careful not to squeeze too hard and frighten her. "You don't have to ask, sunshine. The lap is all yours whenever you want it."

*Not if I get there first.* The thought popped into Belle's head and she had to hide her face, worried that her odd reaction was there for him to read.

# Chapter 6

Jesse started the next day full of plans. First, he intended to get the critters' needs dealt with, fresh water and food dishes filled. Then a long walk with Sam to deplete some of the pup's excess energy.

The two overly large white Persian rugs that Kim called her ladies came running the minute they heard the rattling of the bag that held their food. They meowed and wove their way around his legs, tripping him up when he bent to lower their dishes to the floor.

From the sweetheart called Puff, he received a lick on the hand, and from the bitchy one called Snowball a nip was his payment. *Blasted cat!* Must be her crossed eyes making her moody. He could never figure out if she was looking at him or behind him.

The caress he bestowed on Puff arched her body until his hand worked its way up to the tip of her tail.

The similar touch he tried on Snowball didn't end with the same result. This touchy feline hissed and rewarded him with a scratch from a claw she'd shot out faster than he could react and move.

Sucking his finger he glared at her. "Get your own food from now on, you grumpy thing."

She responded with a blink, a sniff and her fluffy white back turned sulkily in his direction.

The puppy Kim called Sam, a golden Lab that wanted everyone to like him, bounded in between the two cats, and only Jesse's quick reaction saved the pooch from Snowball's temper. Even Puff showed her dislike of this type of shenanigans during mealtime and leaped away from his playfulness.

"My friend, you are living dangerously," Jesse spoke to the enthusiastic pup whose black eyes gleamed with mischief. Head tilted, he waved his paw toward Jesse's cheek then aimed his snout and tried to lick him. "Never mind trying to be cute. Those two monsters could eat you for a snack and still be hungry."

He carried the mutt to the door and retrieved the ridiculous, black studded leash his sister thought suited her pet. "It's time to take you for a walk, so behave." A growl and then a lick from Sam's lunge at his face was his answer.

A little while later, Jesse found that walking a puppy became a lesson in restraint and patience. Not quite grasping the male stance when relieving himself, Sam squatted to pee and then tried to lift his leg at the same time, which just meant he fell over. It would be hilarious if not for the fact that Jesse would have to add bathing the terror to his list of chores.

Trying to keep the leash from getting tangled turned out to be a fiasco. Sam had four goals: sniff everything he could get to, pee on anything higher than a blade of grass, chase whatever moved, and drive Jesse crazy. By the time they got close to home, he'd had enough of the nonsense. While bending to pick up the pest, he heard someone calling his name. He stopped and turned toward the voice and saw Belle walking slowly with Layla running full steam to catch him.

The little girl skidded to a halt in front of him and crouched down. "Jesse. Isn't Sam wonderful?" In his haste to adore her, the terror jumped up and knocked her over on her backside.

"No! He's nothing but a pain." Her giggles and unsuccessful efforts trying to push the furry monster away made her laugh. Finally, Jesse whipped his hand out and nabbed the hyperactive animal.

Glad to hear her giggles, he helped Layla to stand, apologized to Belle, and made unnecessary excuses. "Kim has *got* to find the time to train this beast to behave."

Belle reached out to pet the now frenzied animal and said, "He's a baby, Jesse. There's time enough to train him when his attention span is longer than two seconds."

"Then I'll just have to ground him." Jesse winked at Layla and felt his heart lighten when she thought him serious and said, "He didn't mean to be bad. Did you Sammy?"

Two short barks, sounding very much like the word "sorry", was their answer, and even Jesse had to laugh.

Belle glanced around at the lovely blue sky. "The day called for us to take a walk. I felt well enough and it seemed like a good idea but now I'm not so sure. It's nice to rest for a few minutes."

"Actually, you look slightly better. Those eggs settled your stomach okay?"

"They did. I had more this morning. I searched the internet for meal suggestions and found quite a selection. But that's enough about me. What are you up to this fine day?"

"This and that. I have chores that I've put aside for some time. That always happens near the end of a project. Therefore, I need to get them crossed off my never-ending list."

Jesse saw Layla's face waver, the joy at seeing him

disappearing. Before he knew he would, words flew from his mouth that he'd had no intention of uttering.

"Later, though, I have a property to look at in the Green Lake area. It's where I'm thinking to build my next house. If you're up to it, maybe you and Layla would like to come along for the ride."

"Can we, Mommy? Please!" Layla jumped up and down, clapping her hands. The begging look on her face turned out to be no match for her mom. Jesse certainly couldn't have withstood her manipulation. He waited for Belle's answer... and it surprised him that it mattered so much.

# Chapter 7

Belle knew Jesse had been totally fleeced by her little matchmaking daughter and decided he needed to be let off the hook. That is, until she saw the expression on his face. Watchful and hopeful if she read him right.

"I guess we could come if you don't mind. It'll be nice to get out of the apartment. Thank you for asking us."

Jesse nodded, "Good, I'll come for you around three." He ruffled Yaya's hair and headed in the other direction.

Belle turned and followed his tall figure as he loped across the street, the small pup galloping to keep up. She enjoyed the way the man moved, his hips in coordination with his arms and his well-formed butt swaying in an almost-strutting style.

All too soon, he disappeared through the front door of their building.

Belle's heartbeat had picked up and the dryness

in her mouth had her wetting her lips and sighing deeply. The man's long legs and muscular form would be considered, at the very least, a healthy specimen, and at the very most, deliciously sexy.

Yaya pulled at her mom's hand, a serious expression settling over her little-girl face. "Jesse's so nice Mommy. I love him."

Touched by her baby's declaration, she replied, "He does seem like a very nice man. And you don't really love him, you like him."

"Nope. I *weally* love him." Having had her say, Yaya skipped away to examine a flower growing out of a crack in a brick wall.

It was a blue forget-me-not and the color of the tiny bloom brightened up the greyness of its surroundings. A thought popped in and made Belle smile. Kind of like how her Yaya brightened up her life.

Belle checked her watch and caught her little one's hand. "Yaya, we need to go home now because Kim promised to Skype us today and she'll be connecting in a few minutes. If we're not there, she'll worry."

Within a short time, Belle sat in front of her laptop and smiled into the dazzling green eyes of her best friend. "Hi, Kim! Yaya wants to say hello before her cartoons start."

Belle lifted her daughter on to her lap and

watched while the two devoted buddies had their few moments. Soon she sent Layla to the other room so she could visit with Kim in private.

"How's everything at the shop working out? Will you have to stay there for the whole season or can you place someone else in charge?"

"Hey, my friend! Looks like I'll be here until after the holidays unless I can talk one of my other managers into leaving their families at this time of the year. Which ain't gonna happen."

"Guess not. Well, when you're the boss, it all falls on your shoulders. We miss you. Yaya keeps pestering me about when you'll be home. It shocked her when she found your brother instead of you in your apartment yesterday..." *Whoops! Darn her big mouth!*

Just as she knew would happen, Kim latched on to her words and demanded an explanation.

"Why did she go to my apartment?" With her eyes narrowed and the smile wiped away, Kim meant business. "What happened?"

"Nothing, really. I scared her when I fainted."

"Oh my god! You fainted? She probably thought you were dead, poor baby."

"She did. Got frightened and ran to get you and found Jesse there instead."

A mischievous smile lit up Kim's face before she

asked, "What did he do?"

"He came right over. I had started to come around and felt much better once he'd put me back on the couch. He's a sweetheart, exactly like you said."

"Shame he's not into long term relationships. The man's still nuts over his first love from high school for pity's sake. Her name was Mari Krude and she was every guy's fantasy. Blonde, with big grey-green eyes, a gorgeous figure, smart like the dickens... and, too sweet to be true."

Mari Krude? The name rang a bell for a few seconds but Kim's voice intruded before Belle could pin down the thought. The fog she lived in kept her from being as sharp as she used to be and she hated it.

"What's wrong? You tuned out on me for a minute there. Is your mind still hazy?"

"Some days it's worse than others. I just thought the name rang a bell, but it's gone now. So, was she the Homecoming queen and Jesse the king?"

"Nope. Mari could have been the queen but Jesse was too shy and laidback to care about stuff like that. Popularity didn't matter much to him. Being a bit of a loner, he spent more time on his skateboard than playing football."

"She didn't mind?"

"Guess not. They were tight and nothing got in-between."

"If they cared that much, why'd they separate?"

"Her parents got divorced. Then her mom met another guy, got married again and Mari moved with them to L.A. I guess she and Jesse corresponded for a while but Mari finally broke it off after a year or so."

"That's a bummer."

"I know. Jesse had just graduated. The guy had worked like a dog all summer to save his money. The plan was for him to move closer to her. Then she sent him a 'Dear John' letter saying that she was engaged to another guy."

"That would do it."

"Exactly! I remember the day he got the mail. At first, his face was all covered in smiles from seeing her pink envelope. It turned hard and kinda scary in a matter of seconds."

Kim leaned closer to the screen and Belle caught herself copying her.

"That night, Jesse phoned Mari to try and talk her into seeing him one more time. He never knew, but I snuck by his open window on the patio and listened. He begged and she refused—broke his heart. I heard his grief. It was horrible. My brother never was the same carefree guy after that."

"The bitch!"

"Yeah. That's what I called her and still do. He's

been a recluse for far too long. I've tried to get him to drop the past, to move on, but so far no luck. Speaking of moving on, you look a bit better today."

"Today I feel better than I have in quite some time."

"I can tell. There's more color in your face and your eyes seem clearer. What's changed?"

"Something that Jesse said has given me hope. I researched it all morning and many of the symptoms are close and others dead on."

"What is it? You're making me curious."

"Well, he told me that one of the guys who works with him has a mother who suffered in the same way. He was a bit vague on the details but it turned out that she had Celiac disease."

"That's where a person can't eat any gluten, right? Like an allergy, but worse?"

"Yes. As you know, all I've been living on for weeks is crackers and eggs and milk. Well, both the milk and crackers probably just irritated my already raw stomach."

"Oh Belle, you poor thing. On the other hand, if it *is* Celiac then it's good news. I've been worried that you could have had something much worse. Actually, I'd pretty well decided that if you hadn't found any answers by the time I returned, I'd force you to go to my doctors whether you argued or not."

"By then, I probably would've gone. Yesterday, I'd never have said this, but I will now. I was about as low as I could go."

"That makes me feel sad, Belle." The sentiment showed in Kim's expression.

"Don't be, Kim. Now I have hope. That makes me happy."

Layla raced into the room and yanked at Belle's shirt sleeves. "Mommy, Mommy, Uncle Jack is here."

As Belle took in her daughter's words, the pit of her stomach plunged to the floor. "Don't let him in, Yaya."

"It's too late, I aweady did. I thought he was Jesse."

"Is everything all right, Belle? What's this about Uncle Jack?"

"Sorry, Kim. I can't explain now. I'll e-mail you later."

"You'd better. From the expression on your face, Uncle Jack isn't welcome and I'll have the heebie-jeebies all day until I hear from you."

"Heebie-jeebies?"

"Don't mess with me, pal. You know what I mean."

# Chapter 8

Belle first sent Yaya to her room with a new baby-doll coloring book and crayons she'd been saving as a Christmas present. Then she took a deep breath and went to greet her unwelcome guest.

When she entered, Jack, sitting on the edge of the chair and threading his hands through his messy hair, jumped to his feet. He appeared even more agitated than the day before and didn't seem to know how to start the conversation. He started to speak and then stopped mid-sentence. His eyes wouldn't focus and the day-old beard and rumpled uniform led her to believe he hadn't slept.

Fear took hold and she had a hard time not letting it show. Putting on a brave front, she said, "Jack. Why are you here again? I told you yesterday that we have no future together. Both of us need to move on."

"No!" His hand slashed too close to her face and had her stumbling backward. "I'm not leaving. I belong here with you. I have nowhere else to go, Belle. Please let me stay."

Belle, not wanting to upset Yaya again since she'd had such an upheaval yesterday, tried to soothe Jack. "There's no room here, Jack. It's not possible. You need help. Go to the VA hospital, they'll look after you there."

"I don't want a hospital. We're family, you, me, and Layla. We'll get married and things will be better, I promise. I'll try harder. I can do it if I have someone to look after me."

Shaking her head was merely an instinctive reaction, but Jack took offense. Punishingly strong, his arms swept her into a hold and at the same time, he tried to kiss her. When she resisted, he forced her to the floor and overpowered her with his heavy body.

Struggling without making a sound, a nightmare no woman should have to suffer, Belle tried to get free—which compelled him to exert even more force.

Exhaustion took hold very quickly, but still, she pushed ineffectively at his chest. "Stop it, Jack." She turned her head away from his seeking, slobbering mouth. "You're hurting me." A sob broke free and then another.

Just before his body was wrenched from hers, a

movement from the corner of her eye caught her attention. A furious Jesse grabbed Jack by the collar of his uniform and hauled him off her. He shook him like a dog shakes a rodent, then he frogmarched him to the door and all she heard was his threat. "Get out and don't come back. Or next time, I'll have to call an ambulance because you'll be needing medical attention."

Belle covered her eyes with her bruised arm and rolled to her side to curl up in a fetal position. Mewing like a hurt animal, a noise she couldn't seem to stop, she thanked the good Lord for Jesse's perfect timing.

In seconds, the gentle giant cradled her body while lifting her off the floor. Without any hesitation, her arms wound around his neck and the shudders she couldn't stop affected every bone in her body. Shaken, frightened, and sick at heart, Belle clung and wept.

Finally, cuddled on the sofa in his lap being rocked side to side, she quieted. "How did you know?"

"Kim called. She was worried. Said the look on your face when Layla told you her Uncle Jack was in the apartment scared her silly."

"The news scared me silly also. I can't stay here, Jesse. He'll come back. The man is sick in his head.

He used to be a wonderful brother-in-law and uncle but not anymore. Since he returned wounded, he's gotten worse. I thought we'd escaped him when we moved here, but he found us again. I don't know what to do—"

His hushing stopped her chatter. Shock was making her crazy. She knew it and could do nothing to control herself.

"Don't cry anymore, Belle. You don't have to stay here. Kim has two bedrooms at her place, so you can come and stay there with me. I'm not letting that animal near you again. I don't care how good a guy he was before this happened. He's broken now and needs to get himself fixed."

Belle pushed away from the warmth of his chest to look into his eyes. She searched the grey softness hunting for any signs that his offer made him uncomfortable. Nothing showed, other than caring and compassion and a very faint glow deep inside that made her tremble with delight rather than fear.

He placed a kiss on her forehead and stood up so he could gently lower her to the floor. "Let's get Layla and go for that drive I promised you. We'll stop for dinner at a restaurant I've just heard about that serves a variety of gluten-free meals. Then we'll come home and move what you need down the hall. If you feel worried about having me stay with you, I can always sleep here."

Her female instincts reacted negatively against this suggestion and her shaking head seemed to reassure him. "I want you to remain with us. I'd feel much safer in case Jack finds out that we've only moved a short distance. His army training gave him skills that we can't underestimate."

Obviously joking, Jesse winked and said, "Okay then. Just as long as you promise not to jump my bones, we've got a deal."

Belle hid her grin and kept quiet. No way in hell would she make a promise she had no intention of keeping.

# Chapter 9

Jesse didn't know why it mattered to him that Belle like the property where he'd chosen to build his next house. It had never bothered him before if anyone vetted his choices. By the time he'd finish the construction, there were always people waiting in line to see his work.

Sales were fated since Jesse's reputation as a quality builder had been enhanced by the story written in New Homes, a magazine that featured the most beautiful houses in the Seattle area.

Publishing the story hadn't been his decision. The new owner had signed up for the interview and mentioned him by name often throughout the post.

That had happened three years ago. Now he held a bit of celebrity status that he put up with rather than promoted.

This land, that he'd brought the girls to see today, mattered to him. It had been on his radar for quite some time and he'd been pleased as punch when his real estate buddy had called to tell him he had first dibs.

Belle returned to his side. "It's a fantastic view from up here, Jesse. One can see the ocean in the distance and the forest looks lush and healthy. Anyone lucky enough to have the chance to live here would be very fortunate." Her eyes gleamed with enthusiasm. Her cheeks had taken on a rosy glow from the winter weather and she looked different from the pale creature he'd met yesterday or the distraught young woman he'd held in his arms earlier.

She wandered over to where a small waterfall gurgled over colorful rocks then joined a meandering stream, one of nature's surprising gifts. Happily, she pushed her scarf aside and knelt, cupped her hand, and drank the water.

Jesse couldn't take his eyes off her. Every time he let his thoughts wander back to the sight that had greeted him when he'd rushed to her apartment after Kim's warning, he wanted to scream in fury.

Seeing Belle forcibly held down, covered by the writhing body of a wacked-out sicko, the killer instinct he never knew he possessed woke up. If he hadn't thrown the guy out the door, who knows what he would have done. Scared him just to think of all that rage he'd forced under control. How close he'd come to really hurting the dude.

Layla drew his attention as she danced around on the grassy slope, chasing an ecstatic Sam who didn't know whether to sniff, taste or pee. It had been a good idea to bring the small furball along. His antics had kept them all amused.

Belle walked up to him, laughing at the two babies who were so obviously delighted with their world. "Thank you for bringing us here with you, Jesse. I can see by the proprietorial look in your eyes that the verdict is already made. You're buying it, aren't you?"

"Put the offer in while you and Layla were playing with Sam. It's a site I've been looking at for some time. I might even want to build a house for myself here one day." *Now where did that come from?*

"You should, Jesse. I can see you being happy here, surrounded by all this beauty and peace."

Layla ran toward him, one arm full with a squirming puppy and the other raised so he'd pick her up. "Jesse, can Sam come to the westauwant with us when we go for supper?"

He lifted her and delight escalated when she wrapped her arm around his neck and dropped her tired head on his shoulder. Before he could say no to her question, Belle rescued Sam from her possessive daughter and answered.

"Pets aren't allowed in restaurants, Yaya. It's against health regulations to have animals where food is prepared."

"No, Mama. That lady in the café aw-ways has her big dog with her." The begging in Layla's tone made Jesse grin and try to hide it.

"That's true. But her pet is a seeing-eye dog and she needs him with her because she's blind and he's her guide."

"I can close my eyes and Sam can be *my* seeming-eye doggy?"

"No, he can't be your seeming-eye doggy. He's a very tired puppy and will be happy to sleep in his bed in the car. I promise we won't leave him for very long."

Giving up the good fight, Layla sighed in disgust, snuggled her face into Jesse's neck, and fell instantly asleep.

Jesse chuckled. Who knew a child could drop off so quickly? He watched as Belle settled the sleepy puppy in almost the same position on her chest as he held Layla. "We can get take-out if you'd prefer."

"I think that's best. These sleepy babies would be better off at home. Anyway, I need to pack some stuff for tonight and move it over to your apartment."

"Right! Once you're settled in, remind me to tell you about the woman I met today. Kane's mom, you know the younger fellow who I told you about that works with me. She filled me in on Celiac disease and sent along reams of information from a study she's involved with. I think you might find it extremely informative."

"I'm sure I will. Thank you for thinking of me and doing this."

"No problem. Valerie, his mother, has also invited you to come and see her whenever you feel up to it. She has a lot of recipes she wants to share." As he talked, they walked back toward his parked truck where he set the sleeping child on Belle's knee and took the now passed-out puppy, and tucked him into his cozy carrier.

Handling these domestic actions made Jesse feel lighthearted and happier than he'd felt in one hell of a long, long time.

# Chapter 10

Once he opened the door for Belle and Layla, Jesse watched both their faces. The overabundance of Christmas decorations had bugged him just one day before but now he experienced satisfaction for his sister's fetish of all things Christmas.

Trying to see the room from their eyes made him look closely. The imitation tree itself was huge and glowed from the mass of twinkling lights and other ornaments.

The rest of the room had been similarly adorned. There were Santas and angels and Christmas flowers on every surface, including a wonderful nativity scene that drew Layla like a pond draws the rays of the sun.

"Don't touch, Yaya. The figurines are very fragile and breakable."

Not listening, Layla reached out with her fingers open and accidentally knocked the statue of Mary onto the floor where it broke into a dozen pieces.

Instantly, Layla began to wail.

"Oh Yaya! You shouldn't have touched it, baby." Belle rushed forward, but Jesse reached Layla first.

"Hey princess, don't cry." His arms gathered the heartbroken baby close.

"It was so pwetty, Jesse. I bwoke it. I didn't mean to. I just wanted to see it better." In-between each sentence a wail or a hiccup stressed her uninhibited emotions.

Jesse stood up and cuddled the crying cherub. "We'll phone Kim tomorrow and ask her if she can order a new Mary for the set. Don't fret, sweetheart. It was an accident."

Belle, clearly not quite as forgiving, stepped toward the two and reached for Layla. When Jesse passed her over, she made her daughter look her in the eye so what she had to say couldn't be ignored. "I told you not to touch and you ignored Mommy. That was very naughty."

Layla nodded and hiccupped. "I'm a bad girl."

"Because you didn't listen, you broke Kim's valuable decoration, didn't you?"

"Yes." Layla nodded, her face drenched in remorse.

"Tomorrow when we phone Kim, you will apologize and promise her that you will not touch any of her other ornaments unless you ask permission and either Jesse or I will help you."

"I pwomise, Mama."

"Okay then, let's get you in your pajamas and ready for bed."

Brightening somewhat, Layla asked, "Can Jesse read me a bedtime stowy?"

By this time, Jesse's mushy heart had taken quite a beating. Watching a smart mother reprimand her child wasn't easy on a soft-hearted soul. Observing Belle's body language, he knew it wasn't easy on her either.

He was smart enough to understand that one had to use these moments to reinforce lessons for the sake of the child. No one wanted to let a precious little girl like Layla grow up to be a spoiled brat because her parent hadn't utilized such opportunities.

Not wishing to step out of line, Jesse deferred to Belle by saying, "If your mama says it's okay, I'll read you a story. If not tonight, then tomorrow." Thinking to give Belle an out in case she didn't want to indulge Layla just yet, he waited.

"One short story. And no begging for more. Okay?"

"Thank you, Mama. Layla hugged her mom, her tiny arms squeezing her mother's neck hard, sensing she was out of the doghouse.

"You're welcome, sweetheart. Let's get you settled and we'll call Jesse when we're ready."

After finishing the story, Jesse tucked the little girl into Kim's queen-sized bed and leaned into the arms she held up for his hugs. Holding him in place, Layla whispered, "I'm sow-wy for being a bad girl, Jesse. Will Kimmy be mad at me?" Worry had Layla's eyes watching his closely.

Taking her concern seriously, he answered, "You know what? Kim was the clumsiest little girl I ever saw when she was your age. She broke so many things that she was *always* saying sorry. I bet she'll remember that when you tell her what happened."

"She won't hate me?"

Now where had such a youngster picked up that kind of word? Jesse sighed. "No one could hate a good little girl like you, Layla. Just tell her it was an accident. I guarantee you, she'll understand. Look, I'll make you a deal. If you work with me and help me feed Sam and those Persian beasts for the next few days, I'll pay for the new Mary to replace the old one. Okay?"

Happily, Layla kissed his cheek and replied, "Yes, please."

Jesse left a now happy Layla to her mother and made his way into the spare room he'd taken for himself. His eyes automatically went to the photo he kept on his bedside table and it drew him forward.

Lifting it, he gently rubbed his thumb over the one person he'd given his heart to as a young man. The blonde girl wrapped in his arms had a beautiful smile on her beloved face, a smile he saw first thing in the morning and was the last thing he looked at before he turned the lights off at night.

At the time the photo had been taken, he'd counted himself as the luckiest eighteen-year-old alive. That a girl like Marilyn Krude could want him for a boyfriend, fancy him, and make love with him, went beyond his wildest hopes. Never had he dreamed that someone like her could want a reserved, unpopular guy like him.

Then the last week before she'd left for good, they had finally let their love take them past barriers he'd erected. Respecting her had forced him to keep his horniness under tight control, but it had been her who'd driven them past the point of no return.

She'd practically begged, and he'd succumbed. For seven incredible days, he'd been in heaven. Every chance they got, they spent together in a sexual frenzy. Today, he still relived those moments as being the happiest time in his life.

Placing the eight-by-ten photograph back on the table, he sat on the bedside and clasped his thighs, rubbing his hands up and down. Something felt

different today. The yearning he normally
experienced when looking at Marilyn had faded
somewhat. It scared him and he closed his eyes and
made himself remember their last night together at
the school dance.

She'd stayed in his arms the whole night, wrapped
tight, their bodies glued together, tears making it
impossible to smile. Memories of that painful
parting still tore at his heart and made him catch his
breath. Rubbing his chest at the unhealed, unseen
scars, he left the room, heading to the one person
who'd brought the sun back into his gloomy world.

# Chapter 11

Belle lifted the two fluffy white Persians off the bed one by one and gently nudged them from the room. Not liking this treatment, both spoiled felines tried to get back through the door and were forcibly barred.

"Sorry, Snowball, ain't gonna happen. You'll have to sleep somewhere else tonight." Belle firmly pushed the pet's backside.

A disgruntled meow followed as the cat slinked toward the door of the second bedroom and disappeared.

Belle decided to take a moment to fix her hair, maybe change into a nicer sweater. After all, Jesse looked classy even dressed in tight jeans with his expensive sweatshirts and moccasin footwear. It wouldn't hurt for her to try and look her best.

After her shower, standing in front of the mirror, Belle surveyed the damage to her body from the last few months of poor eating habits. She'd lost so much weight that her slim normal had become almost skinny. Her breasts, that had the tendency to be a bit large, were now just a handful. Her stomach lay flat and the bulge from after Layla's birth had completely disappeared.

Dismayed, she turned away and smeared her body with lotion, and put on her best pair of jeans. A cashmere sweater of soft green—a gift for her birthday from Kim—highlighted her eyes and made them look quite pretty. Scrounging some mascara from the massive pile of makeup left on a tray in Kim's bathroom, she emphasized her lashes and stood back, pleased to see what a difference her small contribution had made.

Her dark blonde hair had suffered most from her recent poor diet and the luster normally noticed was missing. So were the soft natural curls she'd always taken for granted. Good thing that today's style was rather straight and choppy because now she fit right in.

Just as she went to leave the room, she spied a selection of various scents that Kim displayed on a mirrored tray. Her favorite, "Shalimar," sat in front and teased her to stop and spray just a slight amount on the back of her neck under her hair.

Ever since Belle had first smelled the floral and amber-woody scent, when she could afford to treat herself, she'd buy a bottle. Months ago she'd run out and missed the extravagance.

Ready to face Jesse, Belle sauntered into the living room and came to a full stop. He'd also showered. His casual but tasteful outfit, jeans topped with a cobalt-colored shirt that turned the grey of his eyes blue, called on every feminine cell in her body to instant appreciation. His damp reddish-brown hair had been cut short and the disordered style he wore suited him.

Belle had to stop gawking, so she said whatever came to her. "I put the cats out of Kim's bedroom because they insisted on sleeping close to Layla. I'm worried that their fur might make her stuffed up since she has a slight allergy to dust and pollen."

"Not a problem. Those furry fiends are the bane of my life right now. Kim indulges those two beyond reason and they have attitudes that the world revolves around them. Puff, I can get along with, but that Snowball should be turned into a rug."

Belle giggled. "You don't mean that. I can see you smiling."

"Yeah! I'm a softie, but don't let the cat out of the bag."

Laughing together changed the atmosphere to one of relaxation for Belle and she continued into the room to flop on the white leather couch. "Do you have the information you were telling me about, from your friend's mother?"

"It's on the coffee table there in front of you. I'm getting a beer; can I get you anything?"

Belle thought to ask, "Does beer have gluten in it?"

"Huh. Some do, I guess. I don't know. We'll have to find out."

She liked the "we" in his answer. "I'll pass for now and fix some tea for myself later if it's okay."

"Of course it's okay. Make yourself at home here."

"I promise we won't intrude for too long. I'll look for another place in a couple of days, once Christmas is over."

"If you're worried Jack will find you here, you can always stay in my apartment over my shop. There's room to store your furniture there if you'd like until you're settled again."

"I don't think that'll be necessary."

"Then you can just stay here until Kim returns in a few weeks."

Belle felt like a huge weight had lifted off her shoulders. "Seriously? You wouldn't mind?"

"You'd be doing me a favor. Next week I'll be really busy working with the architect, setting up the plans for the new house and ordering all the lumber and materials. Now that I've bought the property, I can't wait to get started. I won't have time to babysit the zoo here." He strode out of the room, her eyes following his tall form with total pleasure. *My God, the man had a sexy walk!*

Giving her head a shake, Belle let her mind wander. She fantasized about what it would be like to have the right to approach him. Wrap her arms around his body, slide in close and kiss him breathless.

Picturing this started the juices flowing and had her crossing her legs and hunching to loosen the pressure on her swollen breasts. Desire swept over her and for the first time in her life, she knew what the word lust really meant. *My goodness!*

Within seconds, she heard him heading back into the room and grabbed the stack of papers in front of her to hold them up. Surprisingly, he leaned over toward her. The breath caught in her throat and she knew her heartbeat stopped and then tripled in speed.

When he took the papers from her hand and turned them the right way up, a blush started from the tips of her toes and took only seconds to arrive at her face. How could a serious-minded young woman, a mother no less, act like such a... a teenager?

# Chapter 12

An hour later, Jesse had not only convinced himself but had Belle persuaded that her whole health problem was the gluten in her diet.

"I'll take you to see Valerie tomorrow if you like," Jesse offered. "She said to drop by anytime."

"That would be nice. But I really must go shopping tomorrow. I gave Layla one of her Christmas presents to keep her out of the room yesterday when Jack came." Belle felt sad when she thought of how few parcels she'd been able to afford for Layla on Christmas morning. Without meaning to, she spoke her worries out loud. "There will be so little under the tree for her."

Jesse's voice held a gruffness that caught her attention. "Kim left gifts for both of you here. And I intended to get something for the munchkin also. In fact, I'd appreciate you helping me chose a present you think she'd like."

"She loves baby dolls and stuffed animals as you

must have noticed since she made you help her pack them all to bring over here. We certainly couldn't leave any behind or they'd be lonesome and *cwy*." Belle pronounced the word in the same way Layla had and made them both chuckle.

Since they'd sat together while reading the papers and hadn't shifted, when she turned his way to share her joke, she found his face close to hers. Their eyes caught and their grins slowly faded.

The intense way he stared made her bones turn to mush. Belle felt herself lean closer as if drawn by the magnetism of his passionate gaze. Heat enveloped her and breathing ceased to function normally. Instead, she held her breath and prayed his lips would find hers soon.

*Glory be!* Jesse finally moved closer and his mouth came within inches of feeding her hunger. A light kiss—tempting, intoxicating, not nearly long enough. As if she were a specimen and he a lab tech, he lifted his head to watch her reaction.

*Enough!* Belle pushed at his chest until she could see his face. "Either you kiss me or you don't, but I'm not a plaything for you to tease." Furious, she tried to stand but found herself lying across his lap as his mouth ravaged hers.

Jesse's lips, punishing at first, softened as soon as he felt her response. Hungry for affection—no, starving—Belle melted against him and prayed he'd never let her go.

As his hands moved under her sweater, Belle accommodated him by twisting so there'd be more space for them to travel. When his lips journeyed to her neck, she arched her head willingly so he could reach every inch. The hardness in his lap poked at her hip and she moved suggestively, as blatant an invitation as she'd ever given in her entire sheltered life.

"Your skin is so soft," he whispered. "I like soft skin."

"Thank you," Belle said, the huskiness in her voice sounding strange. "I use lotion."

Jesse smiled at the same time as his lips found hers once again. "Good idea," he said, seeming to enjoy her naivety.

His tongue delved into her mouth and playfully invited hers into his. She willingly followed and was soon caught up in their little game. But only until breathing became impossible.

Arching forward, her breasts swollen, crying for attention, Belle rubbed her chest against his in an agony of need.

Not too slow now, his soft, warm hands searched and found the aching mounds. Gathering one into his palm, he rubbed the tip and caressed the skin around it, squeezing and stroking. He did the same to the other until Belle felt like crawling up his body so his mouth could reach to where his hands were working.

As if she'd spoken her needs, Jesse drew her down into a prone position where they were lying side by side. Then he undid the buttons of her sweater and pushed each side open so his mouth had full range.

*Oh Lordy!* The man did have a way with his tongue. Belle squirmed in pure ecstasy. Moaning her pleasure, she roamed his back trying to please him as much as possible. When her fingers clawed slightly and scraped his skin, his sighs of pleasure told her she was making him very happy.

Soon she wanted to touch his chest as well and she tugged at his shirt. Taking her hint seriously, Jesse swung away and took it off. Then he undid the button at the top of his jeans and turned to help her with hers. Belle wondered if he noticed her instinctive reaction when she saw his muscular form. The man was beautiful!

Once she lay in front of him in her panties and bra, she held up her arms to welcome him back. Smiling crookedly, his eyes devouring her, he leaned in close to cradle her face. In her ear, he whispered words that broke her heart.

"Mari, are you sure?"

She stiffened. Had she heard correctly? Pushing against his chest, she glared at his confusion. "*I was* sure. But maybe you should ask *Mari* how she feels?"

Scrambling out from under him, slapping at his hands trying to keep her there, she stomped from the room. Every nerve in her aroused body screamed in vexation. *Blasted hell!!*

# Chapter 13

Jesse collapsed on the couch after Belle, furious and with darn good reason, left him to stew in his own stupidity. Shamed by his ridiculous slip of the tongue, he covered his face. *Damn fool!* How could he have treated Belle so shabbily?

The scent of her perfume had permeated the material and he inhaled deeply. The lady had prepared for him, fixed herself up so when she'd first appeared, his eyes had almost popped out of his head. She looked gorgeous in her fuzzy green sweater and jeans that portrayed a body with long legs and a slenderness most women craved.

It was the first time that a woman had taken him to the same intensely emotional place he'd last visited with his childhood sweetheart, Mari. A place where his heart was as much involved as his head.

Scratch that! This time, his head had been buried up his ass. *What an idiot!*

He rolled over on his stomach, trying to calm the

painful ache in his whimpering lower body. Unfulfilled, and deeply saddened, he forced his pounding heartbeats to slow and his brain to kick in.

How in the world could he make this up to Belle? Explain. Apologize. He'd be a fool if he'd ruined his chances with this woman because of a slip of the tongue that he hadn't been conscious of uttering.

Hell, for the first time in forever, a female had caught his interest. He cared. Couldn't help himself. Not only was he keen on Belle, but her little Yaya had also stolen his heart. God, she was a cutie! They both were.

With his befuddled state clearing slowly, he could see them building a relationship where they could work together, create a future, fall in love.

What?

Where had that come from? Other than Mari too long ago to be clear anymore, he'd stayed away from visions of forever-after. Most times he spent with a woman nowadays was for one sweet evening and only one. And he made sure the woman felt the same.

When he let himself remember Mari and the days when they were a unit, he'd known absolutely that she was the only one he wanted. No one else—only her! Every moment of the day she'd lived in his head. Her wonderful sense of humor enthralling him, the way she'd giggled and grinned into his eyes as if only he could share her happiness.

That gorgeous girl had made him feel ten feet tall. She'd adored him and let the world know. For a guy who had trouble talking to others, he'd let her be his voice, his passage into the "in" crowd, his decision maker...

And his heart-breaker.

No doubt about it, she'd broken his heart and his spirit. Nothing ever looked as bright or pretty or simple to him after she'd left and taken his love with her.

Funny thing, it hadn't bothered him before now. Living in his dreams, letting her still rule his whole world, had been okay. Sure, he'd met other women and because they weren't *her*, he had no trouble walking away.

With Belle, he had the sneaky suspicion it wasn't going to be that simple. She mattered to him. Her safety had become paramount to his own comfort.

When he'd suggested she move in with him, he'd been stunned at first. No way would he normally have offered to share his space with any other person, certainly no other female. Thankfully, his protective nature had superseded his old habits and he'd made the offer.

Once he'd heard the words, he knew it was the

perfect solution and he'd mentally patted his back for coming out with the suggestion. When she'd agreed, his spirit had lightened and his relief became obvious. *She mattered.*

So now he had a big problem. He'd begun to make passionate love to one woman, and the name of his earlier lover had slipped out. Was it a Freudian slip? Did he really want Belle to be Mari? In his subconscious, had he switched their identities in order for his heart to be able to get involved?

How the hell did he know? And how could he figure out a reason so he could explain it to Belle?

If she left him now, it would hurt—badly. He knew it like he knew he'd screwed up big-time. So he needed to come up with the right words to explain his stupid behavior, keep her with him, and not scare her by pushing things too fast. Poor girl had enough on her plate without him adding to her burdens.

Giving up trying to make sense of his actions, he headed for his bedroom only to stop at the open door when he spied the two white monster fur balls spread over his pillows.

He growled and had to steel himself not to be angry with them. After all, they weren't to blame that he'd just messed up the best thing that had happened to him in years.

# Chapter 14

Tears obliterated everything in the washroom where Belle hid. Curled up on the floor with her knees under her chin and her drenched face hiding, she let all the despair that she'd fought against wash over her.

Why did life have to be so tough? Just when she thought her world might be getting better... Wham!

Shying away from the reason for her suffering, Belle focused on the recent good stuff. Like reading those notes that Valerie sent about the Celiac symptoms and the treatment that turned out to be so simple. Everything she'd read indicated that as long as she ate the right foods, her stomach troubles would improve, and within a short period of time. All her health worries could turn out to be a thing of the past.

What a relief. She'd be here to watch her daughter grow up and get married. A nightmare she'd lived with when she thought her sickness might be cancer or some other horrible death sentence.

Then not having to deal with Jack all by herself had lightened her load immensely. Knowing Jesse was covering her back, caring about Yaya's and her safety had made the whole ordeal not so scary or intolerable.

Knowing Jack when everyone liked him, when he'd first left to go to Iraq, helped her somewhat to forgive his recent behavior—not tolerate it, but at least try to understand. He needed help. No... he needed to help himself. Overwhelmed by it all, she shied away from those images.

Finally, the thoughts she'd tried to keep at bay flooded in, and this time they wouldn't be shut off.

*Jesse!*

The man who'd attracted her from the first moment he'd lifted her in his arms and held her against the warmth and strength of his solidness. If she could have left her life and stayed there forever, she'd have been tempted to slide inside him and just let the world go by.

Consumed by guilt from her random thoughts, she knew she'd never take the easy road, or leave her precious baby. As a mom, her first responsibility was to the daughter she adored more than anyone else in the world. No one had ever come close to being on the same level of importance.

Until now.

In the beginning, when she'd sensed an attraction growing between her and Jesse, she had to admit to being totally unnerved. Especially once Kim had told her about Mari. The idea of an unrequited affair with a childhood sweetheart as competition freaked her out. How could she compare? And now this!

Sickly, skinny, a daughter to be responsible for, all those entanglements would throw any man off... Jesse included. No wonder the guy got rattled.

*Hold it! Don't give the jerk any excuses.* His behavior stunk. Period!

Shivers worked their way all over her body and made her cling tighter to her resolve not to weaken. Not to let the pain take over. And certainly not to let her heart break.

She sniffed and reached for the toilet paper hanging on the roll next to her face. Unwinding a long piece, she blew her nose and wiped her face.

Enough!

Then she stood up and finished undressing so she could slip into her flannel pajama bottoms and matching short t-shirt. The pants had to be tied tightly so they wouldn't slip off. Next, she ripped the brush through her hair, scrubbed the streaks from her face, and leaned in to brush her teeth.

When the new tears appeared, she leaned forward

to stare at herself in the mirror. *Stop it! That man isn't worth your misery.*

He'd been the fool, not her. He was the one living in the past. And he wouldn't get another chance to play with her again. From now on, they would be strictly roommates, maybe friends, but never again would she trust him with her most tender emotions.

*Never again!*

# Chapter 15

The next morning, Belle blessed Layla's joy at being with her two favorite adults. It helped to dispel the strained atmosphere.

Jesse tried to catch her eyes a few times, but she refused to let it happen. When he tried the throat clearing, she almost gave in but couldn't. Finally, he spoke to her back.

"Belle, I don't know what happened. I'm so sorry—"

She shrugged, and using a flippant voice, she let him off the hook. "Whatever. No biggie." Then she pushed past his reaching hands to get back to the stove and safety. Darned if she'd make it easy for him to embarrass her again.

The despondency on his face gave her a moment's reflection but common sense kicked in. Remembering her resolution from her sleepless night before, she shrugged and continued with breakfast preparations for her and Yaya.

However, not having a vindictive bone in her body, she broke down, ended her silent treatment that had only survived a short while, and asked, "I'm cooking a mushroom omelet for us, would you like some?" When he didn't reply, she turned his way and waited.

After he sneezed a number of times and Yaya happily yelled from her high chair, "Bless you," Belle gave in and asked, "Have you got a cold?"

"No. It's those darn cats and the endless fur flying everywhere. Each time I put them off the bed, they yowled and jumped back on. When I decided enough was enough, I hauled them out and shut the door. I'm surprised their caterwauling didn't wake you and Layla. Only way to get them to shut up was let them return. Finally, I gave them the bed and slept on Kim's chaise lounge."

It surprised Belle when a jolt of glee caught her unaware. Since she'd helped Kim carry that particular piece of ornate furniture from her van to the apartment, Belle knew that the sofa was only about five feet long. Jesse's frame had to be at least six-two. Surprisingly, her mood improved. Guess if she had to have an unsettled night, it felt kinda nice to know he'd suffered also.

"Should've moved to the couch."

"Tried," he grumbled. "The smell of your perfume

wouldn't let me relax."

Happier now, she repeated her offer. "Omelet?"

"Yes, ma'am." The droll tone in the words provided an added thrill.

Sitting together at the table a few minutes later, Jesse outlined some plans he'd made for the day. His voice was tentative and she knew why. "I thought I could take you to the shops and then if you like, we could go for lunch." He watched to see her reaction.

Belle knew there was no way she could stand being in his company for the next few hours.

"Sorry, Jesse. Yaya and I are going shopping alone today."

His gaze dropped to his plate. Red colored his cheeks. Not wanting to embarrass him any worse, she piled eggs and mushrooms on her fork and shoveled it in.

Her need for food had grown now that she knew exactly what she should and shouldn't eat. Because of Jesse, she could at least feed one hunger.

Layla piped up just as the silence stretched past endurance. "Can I go and visit Santa?"

Belle saw Jesse's head swivel toward her and she had the grace to blush for having left the visit so late. "I didn't take her because—"

He cut her off. "Of course not. Darned impossible when you could barely walk." His eyes softened.

"Look at you now."

"I know. Isn't it a miracle? As soon as I stopped eating anything with gluten in it, I could feel my strength returning. My stomach stopped rebelling and the food stayed where it belonged."

Belle beamed his way, unable to stop from sharing her happiness at how much better she felt.

"That's really great." He laid his knife and fork across his full plate and with his elbows on each side of the dish, he threaded his fingers as a platform for his chin. "Belle, it was wrong for me to take for granted that we'd spend the day together. But I could drive you girls and drop you off if you like." If eyes could apologize, his were doing a great job. The bags under his lashes were proof of his sleepless night and his probing stare communicated sincere regret.

Oh no! Didn't he get it? She wanted to get away from any chance of making a fool out of herself. Spending any amount of time in his company would stretch her acting skills to the limit. "I don't think that would be a good idea. We like taking the bus, don't we kiddo?" Belle refused to keep looking at him. She would not back down even though she felt his silent urging.

Yaya looked up, strawberry jam evident on her cheeks and a milk ring around her lips. The sweetness in her grin melted some of Belle's firm resolve. "Yes, Mama."

Belle glanced over and noticed that her mischievous daughter's attention had been focused on the puppy she was feeding her toast to under the table. Rather than reprimanding her, she looked away. After all, even she had a difficult time ignoring Sam's begging eyes.

Another silence reigned, less stressful but still uncomfortable. When she thought she'd scream from the pressure, he said, "A girl's trip, I get it. I guess I could meet up with you later and take you for lunch?"

"Yay!" Layla reached out her arms so he would help her down from her chair; except she wouldn't let him go when he went to set her on the floor. Her tiny arms clung to his neck and she smooched his cheek. "I love you, Jesse"

Everything stopped.

Belle's heart lurched, fluttering so hard she thought it might beat itself right out of her chest. Focusing through the film in her eyes was difficult but once she could finally see straight, she watched Jesse's reaction.

He hugged her little girl back, clearly careful not to hurt the little sprite. Then, his voice husky with emotion, he answered, "And I love you, sunshine."

"Do you love my mommy too, Jesse?"

*Oh my God!* Belle cut in before he could reply. "Time to get your teeth brushed, young lady. We need to get ourselves on the next bus. If we leave too late, the stores will be even more packed."

Wriggling so Jesse would have to let her go, Layla shrieked with delight. "I'll beat you, Mommy. I'm weally a fast bwusher!"

# Chapter 16

Belle hustled Yaya onto the city bus heading downtown and pushed all memories of Jesse's downcast expression from her mind. Today, her health had improved so much that she had energy to spare. Which she'd need, ushering a three-year-old dynamo around the busy stores during her favorite time of the year.

Everywhere she looked, houses were decorated with fancy icicle lights and blow-up Santas and even illuminating reindeer that when dark, would glow against the night sky.

Belle pointed to a particularly older home and said. "Yaya, look at all the green ivy traveling along the red brick on the wall just there. The old house is beautiful decorated with such vivid colors, isn't it?"

"Yes, Mama. I like it."

"Look here; see the blow-up Santa on the lawn? He looks perfect with the bit of snow the kids have packed around him."

"I'm going to see the *weal* Santa today, aren't I?"

Belle grinned. "Not the real Santa, Yaya. Remember, Mommy explained how the real Santa has helpers?"

"Uh-huh. But I'm going to see a real helper, right?"

"Right! Hey little girl, did you see the pink and purple flowers still growing in that yard? Even surrounded with the snow, they've pushed themselves through to get to the sun."

"They're vewy pwetty."

A few more houses passed by until Yaya turned to her, her face lit with interest. "Look at those flowers, Mama. How come they're so yellow?" Yaya pointed to an arrangement of fake fall flowers one intrepid gardener had arranged in a huge pot to sit at their front gate.

Belle hugged the child on her lap and answered with a chuckle warming her voice. "They're yellow because they're sunflowers."

"I like them."

Belle nodded and cuddled to get Yaya's attention. "Baby, the world is so beautiful. If you look close, you'll see it everywhere. There's bad, but the good is so much bigger and better."

Soon, Belle set Yaya on the floor and led her to the exit of the bus, noticing the warm smiles from many of the other passengers. It surprised her at how good their approval made her feel.

Fighting their way to the platform where Santa sat, surrounded by excited, and in some cases, weepy children, Belle wondered if this had been such a good idea.

The jolly fat man dressed in red with a beard that looked to be natural rested on a throne full of red velvet, wrapped gifts and Christmas all around.

Belle followed the rules of etiquette and ushered her big-eyed baby into line. "We have to wait for a little while, honey. The other children were here before us. It shouldn't take too long."

A frazzled mother with two rough-looking pre-school boys swiveled to speak. "We've been here for almost an hour already. This Santa is a slow one."

Belle nodded and carried on a conversation with her new friend about Christmas, children, and shopping while the two small males took it upon themselves to entertain Yaya. The time passed pleasantly enough until they were next.

Santa lifted the anxious Yaya into his arms and the angelic cherub put her arms around his neck and squeezed. "I'm sowwy I couldn't come to say hello sooner, Santa, but my mommy was sick."

The older man whose eyes twinkled and whose face did resemble most of the cartoon pictures she'd ever seen of jolly St. Nick, grinned, commiserating with Belle, and answered, "Sweetheart, I'm just glad you could make it today. Now, have you been a good girl this year for your mommy?"

Yaya looked at Belle questioningly and seemed relieved when she nodded.

"Yes, Santa."

"Since you've been a good girl, you deserve something special. So what can Santa bring you for Christmas?"

"Santa, my mama wants a new husband. She misses my daddy and... and she's lonely. I heard her telling Auntie Kim. So, that's what I weally want."

The golden-haired child nodded with conviction at the fat man in red, her face wreathed in dimples and her eyes trusting.

If the floor could have opened up and swallowed Belle, she would have blessed the escape. As it was, she had to suffer the pitying glances from everyone in the lineup who had heard the little girl's plea.

"Well now," Santa harrumphed, hiding his astonishment, "We'll see what we can do for your mom, but no promises. It'll depend on how good a girl *she's* been this year."

Wide-eyed and serious, Layla answered, "She's aw-ways a good girl. She's my *mom*."

"You have a point there, sweetie. You truly do."

He sent a wink in Belle's direction, which clearly meant *Lady it's up to you!* "Now what does *this* little girl want under the tree Christmas morning?" He poked a gloved finger into Layla's chubby belly and visibly melted under her giggles.

"Could I have a new baby doll? One with a pink dwess, please."

"A pink dress. Got it!"

With a last hug, Layla let Santa lift her off his knee and took three steps forward. Then she turned as if she knew he watched her and blew him a kiss, her newest trick. Not surprisingly, she received kisses in return from not only Santa but the helper by his side handing out candy canes, Mrs. Santa.

As Yaya ran toward her, Belle could have sworn she heard his HoHoHo sound a lot huskier than earlier.

While Yaya had been visiting with her favorite character, Belle had spotted the exact doll she'd described to Santa. Not only did the baby doll have a pretty pink dress, it also had a cradle, a sweater set, and tiny slippers to match.

Instantly, Belle realized it would be the perfect gift for her baby. She sidled closer, pointing out various stuffed animals to keep Yaya happy, while she paid specific attention to one particular fact, the price. Once she decided it would fit her budget, Belle sneakily assessed the quality. Since they hadn't spent any of their precious cash on a lot of food for the last while, she still had the budgeted money stashed away. It would be close to the price listed for the doll.

Heart accelerating, thinking of Yaya's happy face Christmas morning, she looked around to see where her little girl had wandered.

# Chapter 17

"She's missing?!" Jesse forced the words out in as normal a voice as he could manage. "Calm down, Belle." *Easy to say, not so easy to do!* His heart sped up to where it made swallowing damn near impossible. Muscle spasms racked his stomach and he had to force composure into his voice. "She's there somewhere, probably just wandered off to check something that caught her attention. You've got a photo of her on your phone. Show it to the employees. Maybe they'll remember seeing her. Meanwhile, I'm on my way and I'll be with you in a few minutes."

Driving like a fiend, Jesse broke every speed limit and even ran a few red lights. He couldn't help it. Just the thought that Layla might have been taken by some wacko pedophile ripped his insides to shreds.

Burning low and deadly, anger created fear that formed horrific images and ended in avowals. He'd kill anyone who hurt that beautiful angel. And no one would blame him.

*Stop it! Get it together before you see Belle. You won't be any good to her if you're a mess.*

By the time he ran toward his hysterical roommate, he knew Layla hadn't been found. Belle threw herself into his arms, her face twisted in misery. Tear tracks and pain changing her green eyes to grey pools of sorrow.

The manager, who'd been notified by the clerks dealing with Belle's mounting hysteria, continued placating her by saying this happened quite often and they always found the young culprits.

Turning to Jesse, he added, "Kids move faster than greased lightning when it comes to this store, Sir. I'm guessin' they can't help themselves. It's all those toys to excite them, especially during this season. They forget about Mommy when they get into wandering and looking. Next thing they know, they're lost."

Jesse patted Belle's back while keeping her tucked inside his arms and said, "Has *anyone* seen her?"

Clearing his throat, the heavy-set man admitted, "Not yet. I've sent the photo to some of the department heads to keep a lookout. In the meantime, we're announcing her name over of the loudspeakers every few minutes, telling her to go to any salesperson and tell them who she is."

"Do you have video surveillance throughout the store?"

"Well sure, but it won't come to that. It's only been a short time. She'll show up." The man took a call on his cellphone, giving Jesse time to speak with Belle.

He eased her from his arms and wiped her cheeks with his bare hands. "You looked around on this floor, no doubt?"

"Yes. It was the first thing I did. I called so loud; they came to shush me. That's when I called you. Then the manager appeared. Do you think he's right, Jesse? Could she have just wandered off and is lost now?"

"Why? What are you saying?"

"She's never wandered off on her own before. Never! In fact, she has a thing about me being out of her sight. I guess that's why I let go of her hand. I've always been able to trust her." By the end of the speech, tears overflowed again and Belle had lost the ability to speak.

Jesse reached for the tissues that the salesgirl nearby passed over and used them to wipe Belle's face. "Where exactly were you when she went missing?"

Belle moved to the left and pointed to the display where she'd looked earlier just before Layla had disappeared. "I came here to check these out for her as a Christmas present." Belle picked one of the pretty toys up. "Yaya loves baby dolls. She asked Santa for one with a pink... a pink dwess."

At this point, Belle's voice broke. Trembling visibly, she rocked the doll back and forth, like one would with an infant. Emotions rigidly held in check wreaked havoc with her expressions. With her chin quivering and her voice barely understandable, she continued, "See this one has the pink dress. Oh *God*, Jesse. I only turned away from her for a few seconds."

The manager approached; his demeanor not very promising. "I've called the police, folks. It's policy, so don't go getting too frantic. They'll put out an Amber Alert throughout the city just in case she's left the store."

***

Questions and more questions had Belle close to a nervous breakdown. The police had interrogated the salesclerks, who didn't remember seeing Belle or Layla. Thankfully, Santa and his helper remembered her very well.

"That little girl made a real impression, officer. She was sweetness wrapped up in a fuzzy purple hoodie with a white pompom on the top. She bounced with energy and had the cutest smile matching the prettiest green eyes I've ever seen."

Thinking she had no more tears left, Belle broke down again from the portly man's description. She noticed that even Jesse's chin wobbled slightly before the muscles in his cheeks signaled he'd clenched his jaw.

The police precinct, not a place anyone wanted to spend a lot of time, bustled with everyday commonplace drug addicts, assault victims, hookers, and criminals, all with a multitude of stories.

Waiting to be called for her statement, Belle watched the down-and-out folks from around the city living what to them would be a commonplace experience and what to her was a nightmare.

One man dressed in camouflage became particularly belligerent. It took two cops to subdue him and Belle felt her heart go out to the loser, one who'd likely served his country.

"Mrs. Foster? Belinda Foster?"

"Yes!" Belle turned to the policewoman standing nearby.

"Can you come with me please? Officer Todd from Missing Persons would like to ask you some questions."

Belle, who'd clutched Jesse's hand from the minute they'd arrived at the station, went to draw him with her.

"You go and tell them everything, sweetheart. I

have a few calls to make. If I'm not around when you're finished, wait for me here."

Belle nodded. Fear coated every emotion so that thinking became an effort. Moving became a struggle. And breathing became work, hard work.

Leaving Jesse behind took courage, but she had no choice. His smile encouraged her to follow the other woman and the kiss he'd left on her knuckles was now embraced by her other hand.

# Chapter 18

Jesse had noticed a disturbed fellow, dressed like a soldier, and an idea surfaced that wouldn't go away. Moving quickly, he called his old army buddy, Captain Phil Reid, a man totally immersed in helping returning veterans who had trouble with the system.

Jesse begged Phil to check their files for an address for Jack Foster. It wasn't until he came clean as to why he needed the information that Phil agreed to help. On one condition. That he came along to make sure Jack got treated properly.

"No problem, Phil. You'll be able to handle the dude a lot better than me. Right now, if he has Layla, all I want to do is hurt the sick son-of-a-bitch."

"See, that's why I need to be there. I'll text you where to meet."

A few minutes later, Jesse received the address, jumped in his truck, and headed to the nearby street. As promised, he waited for Phil to pull up behind him and exit from the specialized van that accommodated his wheelchair.

Jesse leaned down so they could embrace like men who respected each other tend to do. Hands gripped and a side nudge that meant they were pleased to meet up.

"I checked your boy out. He's a good one, Jesse. Jack Foster served two tours in Iraq, and not the easy missions either. This soldier won the Medal of Honor for bravery and he headed up some important missions. I mean, he stepped up, didn't sit back letting others do the dirty work. His men liked and respected him. Too bad his latest injury seems to have dealt him a hard blow."

"If he's kidnapped Layla, I'll deal him a hard blow." Jesse clenched his fists, hope and fear warring inside like two antagonists both wanting to win.

"Let's just see if he has her. Or if he's hurt her. Then we can decide what happens next. One thing I can promise, from what I read in his file, this man has gone through hell."

Jesse glared down at his friend riding beside him. He respected Phil, always had. From the days when they'd skateboarded as teens to when he'd visited his buddy in the V.A. Hospital after he'd returned from active duty minus the ability to walk, Jesse had cared about and valued his friendship.

"Don't talk to me about hell, Phil. Do you know what Layla's mom has gone through? Belle's just gotten on her feet after being ill for a long time and now she has this nightmare to deal with. I'm sorry, but this takes precedence in my mind."

"Sorry, Jesse. Of course, you've a reason to be pissed."

"Darn right, I'm pissed. Look, Jack's brother Terry was her husband. They lost him a couple of years ago. Now Jack seems to think she belongs to him. That she has to look after him. This sicko physically attacked her yesterday. I had to rip him off her. She was terrified. I'm talking to the point where her fear has forced her to move in with me."

"Okay. I get it. The man's unhinged. But you have to understand, Jesse. He's just a lost soul. We can help him as long as he agrees to rehab."

Not wanting to hear anymore, Jesse demanded, "What apartment is he in?" He moved in front of the wheelchair to the main entry, opened it, and then hurried to push the elevator buttons.

"It's suite three-zero-two."

Once standing to the side of the door, jaw gritted and hands sore from being clenched, Jesse sent up a quick plea to those that watched over souls who needed heaven's help. *Please!*

Phil knocked. He grinned toward the peephole

and waited. The chain stopped the door from fully opening. "What do you want?"

Phil answered, no hesitation at all. "Jack Foster? Hey man, came to pay a call and get you signed up with the Veterans association. Your file has finally gotten to the top of the pile."

"Busy today. Can't talk." Jack's uneasiness filtered through straight into Jesse's worry.

"Sorry, dude. It's important that we converse today. Can I come in?"

"No! I have chores. I'll come and see you next week. Just leave your card." Jack opened the door wide enough to thrust his hand out and that's all Jesse needed. He gave a mighty shove and entered. The first room, dingy and overlooking a busy freeway, left a lot to be desired.

"Get out of here. You can't come busting in like this." Jack started toward him.

Jesse heard Phil try to calm the guy down while he pushed past, through another door, and into a small bedroom. His heartbeat hard, painfully hard, a rhythm that made him want to clutch it and squeeze.

*God Please!* The words shrieked in his head and he had to clench his jaw to stop from letting the screams spew out his mouth.

The unmade twin-sized bed in the corner drew him, but it lay empty. He spun around, searching every corner of the room hoping to see some hint that Layla was either here or had been.

Dammit! There was nothing.

Dragging his feet, Jesse stepped into the other room where Phil had Jack sitting at the kitchen table and obviously schmoozing him about joining the specialized VA group Phil headed up.

Jesse, a good judge of character when it came to men, held back and watched rather than rushing up to grab the guy and beat the living bejesus outta him the way his instincts encouraged.

As soon as Phil spotted Jesse hovering, he asked the necessary question, "So you haven't seen your little niece today, have you Jack?"

"I already told you, no. And what the hell is *he* doing here?"

Phil ignored the question, plowing straight ahead. "Were you home all day?"

"Ahhh yeah! I haven't left the apartment."

Nervous-looking, maybe from his medical complications, Jack's foot tapped as if in time to music only he heard. His uniform shirt and tie, newly ironed and spiffed up, looked quite presentable but it didn't calm Jesse's apprehension. In fact, it made it worse. Why did a man who swore he hadn't left his apartment look so well dressed?

"If you've been home all day, why are you wearing

your uniform?" Jesse cut into the conversation, his voice a lot harder than Phil's. The tone upset the man being interrogated.

"I don't have to answer to you guys. Get the hell outta my apartment."

Now, if Jack would have put some expression into the words, screamed them instead of speaking low, Jesse might have recognized innocence and justified anger but all this speech did was make the hairs on the back of his neck dance in dread.

Dammit all to hell, what was he missing. Something! But what?

Jesse checked his watch and knew he'd been away from Belle for more than an hour. If she were alone without anyone to keep her calm, she'd be a mess, even worse than her brother-in-law. Again, Jesse zeroed in on Jack.

Sensing the other's edginess, knowing with everything in him that they were right about this man absconding with Layla, Jesse decided to take another approach.

"Belle is crying, Jack. Her heart's about to burst from fear of what Layla could be suffering right now. The horrible mind-pictures of who could have stolen her baby are making her real sick. It's ripping her to shreds and you know she hasn't been well lately." While delivering this speech, Jesse watched closely and saw the regret on Jack's face as if he were wearing a huge neon sign on his forehead.

Guilt and regret!

*Holy hell! The closet!* He spun around, ran into the bedroom, and searched for the entrance. Jack's frenzied holler followed him. "No! Don't!"

Sure enough, there was Layla. Curled into a tiny ball on a fuzzy brown blanket, she lay with her eyes closed and her body limp.

Shaking, adrenaline pumping, scared out of his mind, Jesse knelt down and put his face next to the lips of the tiny sprite. He felt her breath and every prayer he'd been whispering turned into a moan of pure gratitude.

Jack and Phil had trailed him and were holding back while Jesse lifted her to his chest and cuddled the precious weight.

"She's sleeping," Jack moaned. "Don't wake her up. Poor baby's tired."

"She's not sleeping normally, Jack. What did you give her?"

Jesse couldn't wring the jerk's neck with Layla in his arms. Instead, his eyes warned Phil to take over.

"Hey buddy, you have to tell us what you gave her. We need to know if she's in danger so we can help her."

Jack's stare swung from Phil to Jesse and then back

again. "What are you talking about? It's only a mild sleeping pill. I'd never hurt Layla. She's Terry's child."

"Calm down, man. We didn't mean anything."

"Listen to me. I loved my brother and I love his family—my family." By now, Jack had seemed to deflate. He sunk to the floor, wracked with tears. "I only wanted her and Belle to live with me. I needed them to keep the blackness away. Don't you see? They're the only ones who love me."

Jesse's anger deflated somewhat as his knees gave out, but not completely. It wasn't easy seeing a man he'd normally want to respect sink so low, but Jesse had to remember that this guy wasn't well. Jack's head was all screwy and he needed help, not hatred... and certainly not pity.

Phil slipped from his chair and sunk to the floor next to Jack, gathering him close. "Hey bud, let *me* help you instead. Belle and Layla need a healthy brother and uncle to welcome home and right now you need some medical and psychological attention to be that guy again."

Jack's hand squeezed his mouth and he rubbed hard as if trying to stop from speaking his thoughts out loud. Jesse knew he'd never forget his words and maybe one day, he could forgive the man for the nightmare of the last few hours.

"I was terrified to be alone. And Yaya still smiled at me. I'd made up my mind that either I spent time with her or I'd give up and give in to those incessant voices urging death as my best choice. I chose Yaya."

Jesse backed away, cuddling Layla. Blanketed in brown fuzz and sleeping peacefully, she looked like a little angel. His heartfelt message of appreciation, obvious in the nod of his head and the mouthed 'thank you' he sent Phil's way, covered his goodbyes.

Once in the truck, Layla snuggled in the back, strapped in as best as Jesse could without a proper car-seat, he searched for his phone. Not finding it anywhere on his person, he realized he'd left it behind. It must have slipped out of his pocket when he leaned over to pick up the babe. For one split second, he thought to go back... and instantly knew he couldn't. Getting Layla to her shattered mom took precedence right now to even breathing.

# Chapter 19

Belle didn't know why Officer Todd asked her the same questions over and then over again. Some he'd repeat exactly and others he'd couched in different terms but Belle wasn't stupid.

Scared and sick at heart, yes, but her faculties were kicking in with a clearness that surprised her. It was all about giving them the help they needed to find her Yaya.

"I've told you; she didn't like being out of my sight. Especially in the stores where there were a lot of strangers. I have no idea why she would wander away."

The uniformed officer who had been assigned to Belle's case, a younger man with his shirt sleeves rolled up and his tie pulled loose, ticked off something on the page in front of him. His desk, piled high on both sides with files and papers and coffee mugs stained from cold coffee, looked as if it hadn't seen a duster or a wet cloth in months, if ever.

But the man sitting behind it had a heart. If it hadn't been for the softness around his smile, she'd have screamed her frustration and swiped the desk clean in the festering rage from her failure to keep Yaya safe.

"Her sweater was purple with a white pompom attached to the hood."

"Before, you said it was a hoodie?"

*Argrr!* "I said it was a hoodie, yes, because it was made in a hoodie style. But I knitted it for her from wool. So even though I used the hoodie pattern, it was also a sweater." Belle felt like she was explaining the facts of life to a grown male who should know better. "Does this *matter?* You've asked me that already."

"Sorry, Mrs. Foster. We have to make sure and get every detail correct. I understand that you're frustrated but know that while we're here going over the details, there are officers all over the city of Seattle looking for Layla."

Belle gripped her fingers yet again and ignored the aching knuckles and raw cuticles. "I'm sorry, Officer Todd. It's just that she's such a baby. I told you, she's scared of men. If a strange man has taken her, she'll be terrified. She'll wet herself..." Bell, overcome once again, helped herself from the same box of tissues he'd passed her way numerous times already.

The door to the cell-like room opened and the same woman who had brought her here advanced with a sheaf of papers in her hand. The two officers held a whispered conference, and the woman left the room, sending a commiserating smile Belle's way.

"Sorry, Mrs. Foster. Look, don't upset yourself with wild scenarios. Let's continue with the questions. You say she was born on February 7th, 2010?"

"Yes. She's almost four."

Officer Todd held one of the new file sheets. "Did she know her father? You told us he was killed in Iraq?"

"Yes, a week before her first birthday. No, she never knew him."

"Do you have pictures of him around the house, maybe in a uniform?"

"Yes, there's one in my bedroom. She likes to look at it and ask questions about her daddy."

"Are your husband's parents alive?"

"No. He lost them some time ago in a car accident. He has a twin brother who's been unwell and who we don't see very much."

Belle wiped the continuing stream of tears and blew her nose for the umpteenth time. She sensed a new direction to his questions and couldn't stop herself from asking, "Have you gotten a lead?"

"Nothing concrete, I'm sorry to say. But we're following every tip that comes our way. Many times, folks come forward once they hear the news and that information helps solve many cases."

"I'm praying that'll happen for Layla."

Officer Todd stood and walked around the desk. He reached out with his right hand and helped Belle to her feet. "I'm sorry we had to meet under such frightening circumstances, Mrs. Foster. But let me assure you that our office is doing everything in our power to get your little girl back. If you'll step into the waiting room again while I make a few calls, I'll get back to you soon. Please."

Belle limped out of his office and found the ladies room where she tried to make herself look presentable. The unkind mirror presented her blotchy face, limp hair that stuck out everywhere it shouldn't, and haunted eyes with no hint of sparkling green anywhere. Just grey misery.

She held cold water-soaked paper towels to her face and tried the deep-breathing technique, forcing in the first profound breath she'd experienced since she'd looked around only to find Yaya missing.

Within minutes, she entered the waiting area only to find Jesse hadn't yet returned. Missing his common sense, his strong conviction that Layla would be found, and the warmth of his nearness,

Belle sunk into a chair. She checked her phone once again in case she'd somehow missed a call. Nothing!

A scream from the other side of the room caught her attention. A young woman dressed in cheap revealing clothes, swore at the cops like a hooker in an R-rated movie. It seems she took offense to the fact that they were charging her with a crime. Struggling, she put up a heck of a fight before they led her through double-doors that made Belle think of the entrance to hell.

Time passed slowly and her stomach let her know it hadn't fully healed. Pain radiated from her chest to her lower tummy, the same symptoms that had made her rush more than once to the nearest bathroom. Finally, dehydrated from fluids and emotion, she collapsed in the chair once again.

A movement to her right caught her attention. From a distance she watched a man approach, carrying a bundle wrapped in brown over his shoulder. The package hid his face.

Her heartbeats picked up and almost choked her. There was something in the way he moved that made her bolt upright. Once he got closer, she could see the fuzzy blanket looked to be sheltering the form of a child. The man seen through the glassed-in walls could be Jesse. The sob caught in her throat while a prayer formed in her heart. *Please....*

As he approached the entrance to her area, the man swung the child to his other side and smiled directly at her. Now Belle was sure.

Sometime later, she swore her scream of joy must have blown out everyone's eardrums, but Jesse defused her of that worry. He said that even though her mouth had been open, she hadn't actually uttered a sound.

# Chapter 20

Back in Kim's apartment with Yaya still sleeping, snuggled up on her lap, Belle couldn't believe the amount of time that had passed from when they'd left the apartment earlier to now.

She glanced around at the warmth of the room; the twinkling Christmas ornaments and the cats who'd somehow sensed her turmoil and were now resting on the floor near her feet. Being spoiled, Sam the pup whined and begged to be picked up by Jesse who'd just entered from the kitchen.

"Jesse, honestly, it seems like days have gone by since this morning. I mean nightmarish days where I couldn't let my mind wander because it wanted to take me to horrors where I knew I shouldn't go."

Jesse stroked Layla's hair one more time as he lowered the mug of hot chocolate and a platter of chicken salad in front of Belle. "Let me take her so you can put something in your stomach and get rid of the chills. I promise to pass her back as soon as you finish eating."

"No, I can do both. It'll be days before I can let her out of my arms."

"Not such a good idea, Belle. I don't think Jack scared her, not really. But you would if you start acting strange. He seemed to have handled her quite well if the shape he was in is any indication. When we arrived, he looked like a soldier should, all spruced up in his uniform, hair cut short and shoes shiny."

"I don't want to talk about that animal. I wish you'd have told me he'd taken her at the police station so I could charge him with kidnapping. How could he have done such a thing?"

"I didn't tell you on purpose. And I gave the information to Officer Todd under duress. Even then, I only passed on my friend Phil's number so they'd have to deal through the Army with him as Jack's advocate."

"Why?" Belle had finally set Layla down on the sofa next to her so that the child's head lay on her knee. She picked up her plate of food to nibble. "You were the one who wanted to take Jack apart when he attacked me the other night. Now you're standing up for him. I don't understand."

"Belle, you're angry at what he did and I don't blame you. But the man is desperately sick and needs a lot of help. If he'd have come home with cancer, I have no doubt you'd have been nursing him. Well, PTSD is just another form of a debilitating sickness. Fortunately, Phil understands these men and with help might be able to get Jack back to where you'll be able to recognize him as Terry's brother, the man you used to care about."

Belle stared at Jesse and let the emotions rampage inside her at his words. Hate had built up for the individual who had taken Yaya, hate and an incredible desire to hurt the animal.

When she'd learned the truth, the hate had faded only to be replaced by all-consuming, fierce anger. Anger that made her want to lash out, to hurt back.

Listening to Jesse's words while caressing her baby's unruly golden curls, Belle stopped to think about what he'd just said. She glanced down at the flushed baby cheeks of the child who had stolen her heart from the first moment they'd met in the delivery room.

Long eyelashes, surprisingly quite dark, fanned against the tiny wrinkles of pudginess. Overwhelming love whooshed around the same place where Belle's devotion existed.

The nurse, called in by the police earlier, had assured Belle that Yaya would wake up in the morning totally refreshed. The deep sleep, though not normal, wouldn't harm her in any way. Still, Belle begrudged that Yaya had had to go through the trauma at all. And not hearing her speak more than a mumble added to her worry.

On the other hand, Jack hadn't hurt Yaya, or at least, she didn't think so. If that were true, maybe she could forgive him eventually. For her husband Terry's sake, a man who loved his brother and was loved back, she had to at least try.

Jesse softly whistled to get her attention. Her mind had wandered and she hadn't spoken since Jesse had sensitively defended Jack's actions. "I'm glad he'll get the help he needs, Jesse. I have to admit to feeling bad because I couldn't help him myself and he is family. Guilt has eaten away at me for months, but the Celiac got there first and I hardly had the strength to care for myself and Yaya. I guess I couldn't cope with two sicknesses at the same time."

"No one could expect you to. But now Jack's in a good place where they understand what he's gone through. They'll be able to help him make the adjustments he needs to get healthy. There's a range of medications that they'll introduce him to which will most likely work to give him back his life."

"Aw Jesse, you're forcing me to remember that I used to love him before he frightened me, before he threatened me. That he's still the same man hidden inside his broken mind."

"He is, Belle."

"You want me to forgive him."

"Not so much!" Jesse stroked the sleeping pup sprawled over his lap. "I want you to forgive yourself."

# Chapter 21

Jesse woke to the delightful sound of Layla's chatter, rolled over in his warm but empty bed, and soaked in the child's delight at being with her mom.

Since he'd purposely left his door ajar the night before in case Layla awoke frightened from her experience, he overheard their conversation.

"Mama, while I waited for you to come and get me at Uncle Jack's he colored pictures with me and made me a peanut butter sandwich. Then when I got tired, he wead me lots of stowies. Uncle Jack's a nice man, isn't he?"

"I guess he is. Though, he should never have taken you away from Mommy because it scared me when I couldn't find you. Layla Foster, look at me. You must never leave me again without asking me first. Do you understand?"

Jesse pictured Layla's big eyes working her mother and knew Belle would melt from the child's endearing habit.

"Yes, Mama. Even if Jack tells me we have to buy you a surprise pwesent, I pwomise I won't go away."

Now Jesse imagined a big puddle of mommy-madness melting off Belle. Sure enough, when he heard her chuckle he knew she'd twisted up inside the same way he felt his own innards reacting to Layla's words. Little monkey knew just how to play them both.

Not wanting to stay away from his girls any longer than he needed to, Jesse started to throw the covers back and stopped dead. His girls? He fell back on the bed. Where the hell had that come from?

Uncomfortable ideas escalated. Visions of a built-in family—wife, child.

Oh. oh, time to clear his head, which he soon found wasn't easy. All through showering and getting dressed, he contemplated where his subconscious had taken him and the more he revisited it the happier he began to feel.

No doubt about it. Layla had crept into his heart, made a warm little nest there, and never 'as in forever' could he imagine evicting her. Thinking about that little cherub lightened his outlook on everything he considered important.

Belle was a different matter. Every time he contemplated romance; his mind jumped to the past. He veered away from letting sentiments, other than pure lust, get anywhere near him.

Being a healthy male, he'd certainly hooked up with women from time to time to satisfy his needs. However, other than Mari, no one had ever gotten past those inner barricades.

Was it time to lower those walls? Did he want to? Nerves attacked his stomach, almost bending him in half. Was he crazy to think of taking another chance? Before he even realized what he was doing, he found himself striding back and forth across his room while fantasies of life as a husband and a father grabbed hold.

Once they got out of hand, he stopped in front of the wall mirror.

Just let things evolve naturally. Stop being a jackass about the future and live for today.

Okay, got it. He'd go out there and enjoy the company.

# Chapter 22

"After breakfast, we'll gather our stuff and move back into our apartment." Belle made the announcement while Jesse was teasing Yaya about sliding in the non-existent snow. She watched his eyes narrow and come close to glaring his reaction.

"You're moving back to the other apartment? Why, Belle? Kim has Christmas all set up here and it's only a few days away. Stay."

Yaya did her imitation of a spoiled little girl by wailing. "I don't wanna go home. I wanna stay with Jesse." Even her lip got in to the act as it began to quiver while her eyes filled.

Belle slowly put down her cereal spoon, looked from Jesse to Layla, and then glanced at her fingers as they rubbed at a milk-spill on the table.

"Layla, honey, this is not our home." Stopping her fidgeting, she reached for her little girl's hand and was shocked when it was pulled back. "We live two doors down the hall, baby. Now that... ahhh, certain matters have been settled, there's no reason for us to be away anymore."

"Couldn't you just stay one more day while Layla and I start to train Sam? Then I hoped we could go together to the mall. Figured while I looked after Layla, you could have time to do *your* shopping."

Jesse sent a mental message to Belle with a wink to accompany it. *The baby doll!* She still had to buy Yaya what she asked Santa for or she'd think she wasn't a good little girl. And that wasn't at all the truth.

With Belle sick for so many months, her munchkin had been an angel, trying to help her as much as possible. She'd gone way past what a normal three-year-old could be expected to handle. Many days, she'd dressed herself and even got her own breakfast and lunch under Belle's supervision.

"Mama, I'll be so good. I pwomise I'll stay with Jesse and hold his hand all the time." Now she had Yaya's pleading eyes to try and resist.

And Jesse's voice wouldn't stop tempting. "After, we could go to the doggy Christmas movie at the Cineplex that I know Layla would enjoy, and then—"

"Oh Mommy, please! Can't we *please* stay with Jesse?"

Belle hardened her heart to the pleading. "We have to get back to our own place, Layla. I still need to decorate our tree and the living room for the holiday."

Jesse broke in, thinking fast. "Look, why don't you and Layla stay here with Kim's decorations all around? If I'm bothering you, I'll hang out at your place or I can get a room at the hotel down the street. Kim wouldn't mind. After all, as long as the herd gets fed and Sam has his walks, she'll be happy."

"Jesse, I couldn't think of putting you out of your home." *Oh, God! Did he realize how tempting his suggestions were? Or how much she longed to stay with him and never leave?*

Tension in the room built until a little girl couldn't take the pressure anymore. Bursting into tears, Yaya settled the issue by flinging herself toward Jesse. He lifted her from her seat and cradled her against his chest. Over her head, his gentle eyes implored Belle to give in, change her mind and throw her heart into a paradise full of delicious torment.

"Fine. We'll stay for one more day."

"Yay!!" Layla and Jesse yelling their satisfaction together broke into laughter and Jesse wiped away Layla's tears.

Belle stood to get their attention. "Just so you both understand. Today, I'll do my shopping and get what we need for Christmas, and tomorrow we move back home. Is that a deal, Yaya? You have to promise me there'll be no more arguments or tears?" Belle raised her eyes and noticed the wary look in Jesse's. "Both of you need to promise."

Layla answered first. "Okay, Mommy."

Jesse took his time and finally, her pointed finger gained his reply. He wore a cheeky grin when he finally spoke.

"I pwomise!"

# Chapter 23

When they finally returned to the apartment, Belle held Layla in her arms while Jesse carried the rest of the parcels.

She imagined anyone looking would think they were a happy family. And that's exactly how they'd spent their wonderful day, just like many of the other contented parents with excited children.

Carrying a sleeping Layla to her bed, Belle knew the smile she'd worn all day was still plastered over her face and firmly lodged in her heart.

Jesse had gone out of his way to make their time together so wonderful that she knew the memory was forever firmly lodged. He'd handled Yaya with such finesse and tenderness that her baby absolutely glowed from all his attention. Most likely, she herself suffered the same pleasant ailment.

In the mall, she'd managed to sneak away and now had a beautifully wrapped present for Layla for Christmas morning that she slid under the ruffled bed skirt. Not only would her daughter get the baby doll, but Jesse had found a delightful doll set with bottles, diapers, fancy clothes, and even a carriage.

Her little girl would be in heaven and the thought lifted Belle so high she felt as if she floated a foot off the floor. Pajamas left under the pillow were soon slipped on to a half-awake grumbler.

"Is she sleeping?" Jesse appeared in the doorway. He'd obviously combed his hair and changed into a clean greenish shirt that exploded the grey in his eyes to appear like emeralds, enticing, appealing.

"The little monkey is still fighting, but she's had it for today. I'll just settle her down and be with you in a minute."

Layla scuttled around her mom's blocking body and held her hand out to Jesse. "I want a goodnight kiss, Jesse. Please?"

He moved closer and Belle got a whiff of his spicy cologne. The fresh scent had her drooling. He leaned over so Yaya's reaching arms could encircle his neck. His first kiss landed on her cheek and another followed for her forehead.

"You smell good, Jesse."

Belle had to admit her daughter had good taste.

"Thanks, precious. Happy dreams."

Belle watched Jesse walk from the room, his swaying hips a pure joy to watch. Bloody hell, the man moved like a model would if advertising sex. And by taking into consideration other women's trailing stares from earlier in the day, Belle had been completely aware that many of the other discriminating females in the mall had felt equally shaken.

Before joining him, she decided that if he freshened up then she would also. Not to impress him—that was dead in the water after he'd called her by another woman's name. But they could still be friends.

With that thought in mind, she showered, fixed her hair, and changed her clothes right down to her underwear. "Whatever!" she whispered the word in the mirror before she joined him in the other room.

"I wanted to thank you again, Jesse, for being so good to Yaya today, in fact, to both of us. It turned into a day we'll never forget."

Jesse passed her a glass of white wine and sat on the sofa across from her. "Trust me, I enjoyed myself as well."

Sam, happy to have his people home again, attacked Jesse's hem on his jeans and began to pull and growl ferociously. Laughing, Jesse picked him up. "Come 'ere you little pest." He laid him on his knees and tickled the ecstatic puppy's tummy all the while Sam tried chomping on his knuckles.

Surprisingly, a chewy treat appeared from Jesse's pocket and Sam, now wreathed in doggy delight, gnawed happily.

He looked at her and smiled crookedly. "Did you hide Layla's present?"

"I tucked it under the bed. She'll never think to look there."

"Maybe not, but if this little monster sees it, he'll be attacking and tearing it to pieces."

Belle laughed. "I never thought about Sam. I'll hide it in the closet then. What made you think of Sam as a destroyer? Come on, I saw you glare at him just now."

"I guess it was the expensive pair of earphones I used to own but are now all teeth marks and dried slobber."

Belle was tickled. "He got you too?"

Jesse put his wine glass down and leaned toward her. "Spill. What did he wreck of yours?"

She couldn't stop the redness that flooded her cheeks. Taking a sip gave her time to wonder if she should mention the panties she'd found on the floor that the little beggar had stolen from her backpack. From now on the zipper would be closed all the way.

"You're blushing. The devil must have gotten into your personal things."

"Yep! And that's all I want to say on this subject.

It'll teach me to zip up my belongings."

Laughing, Jesse stood and wandered over to the entertainment center and turned on some music. With only the Christmas lights on, the room had a sensuous glow. Add the soft music and Belle began to feel tension building inside. What's he up to?

Jesse picked up the bottle, topped his own glass, and approached hers. "More?"

"Sure." By now her body's trembling made speaking difficult. Sipping more wine to try and lighten up, Belle watched him move. Not a good idea if she wanted to remain cool.

"Have you talked to Kim today?" A change of subject seemed appropriate for someone whose insides were flying around like seagulls en mass taking off in the airstreams.

"Yeah. She sent you and Layla her love." Jesse stopped moving and stared at her pointedly as he continued. "And she hoped things were working out between us."

"And? What did you tell her?"

"That I enjoyed having you girls live here and I'd be an idiot if I let you leave." He strode toward her, his hand reaching. "Dance with me." Husky, inviting, his voice lured her in.

Without any conscious intention, she placed her wineglass on the table, stepped into his waiting arms, and was lost.

# Chapter 24

As they swayed, steps matching perfectly, the radio played songs from the past. Jesse happily surrendered himself to Belle's warm embrace. The scent of her perfumed hair brought his body temperature up and his resistance low. She was the sweetest thing he'd held in a long, long... long time.

The arm she placed around his neck was close to his lips. Temptation such as he'd never known before attacked brutally. Not wanting to fight the feeling, he kissed her skin softly and waited for her to reject his advance. She didn't.

Instead, she sighed and arched closer. Without any hesitation, Jesse let her hand go and wrapped both arms around her body which was now glued to his. Bending his height over her, he nuzzled her neck and she twisted, giving him better access. Then he trailed his hand up and down her back as the music carried them to heaven.

Never before had he... His eyes flew open. A song

began to play, an old Elvis song he'd heard years ago at another dance—another time. Memories instantly flooded. He remembered feeling this same kind of aching love just before he'd had his heart ripped to shreds.

Mari's name clanged in his head but he wouldn't make that mistake twice of saying it aloud. Face it, the girl he'd held in his arms back then hadn't been the same as this woman who held him enthralled now. As deeply as he'd loved his teenage sweetheart, she'd left and broken his heart. And as much as he'd mourned her, she'd never returned.

Even without Kim's nagging, Jesse had accepted the time had come to move on. His brain had known it for some time. Guess he'd just waited for the right girl to make it worthwhile to cut those strong ties.

Suddenly, Belle shifted, started to pull away, and he realized he'd come to a full stop and hadn't said anything. He scooped her close again, whispered her name, and heard a distinct sobbing moan.

"Oh, Jesse."

"Belle, I want to kiss you so bad, baby. Let me."

She turned her head, her action the permission he'd longed for. He dove in to taste and lick while his hands wandered her back, her hips, and the cutest butt he'd ever been fortunate enough to have at his mercy.

Whimpers of enjoyment let him know she liked his advances. Being encouraged, he again moved his attention to her neck where his lips played tribute to every inch of her incredibly soft skin.

"Jesse, I love how you make me feel."

In a voice, unlike his usual sound, husky almost rough, he asked, "How do I make you feel?"

"Like a woman." She placed a tender kiss on his lips and gazed into his eyes so he could see her hunger and her truth. "You make me feel like a woman. And it's been such a long time since... No. That's a lie. I've never felt this way."

Her words traveled deep inside to a place in Jesse's soul. A warm, loving place where she now ruled.

Jesse growled his pleasure because words wouldn't form. He picked her up, waited for her legs to circle his waist and carried her to his bedroom. On the way, her lips tackled his, letting him know she liked this direction, promising him a night of intense delight. Carefully, he maneuvered them to the bed, and with their mouths glued in passion, he followed her down.

Belle's hands quickly worked at the buttons on his shirt so he could remove the article. He stopped her from taking off her own silky blouse. Her haste delighted him, making him chuckle.

"Honey, let me," Jesse said. While she watched, he

undid one button, kissed the skin hello, and moved on down till he reached that last one at her waist. Once she lay open to him, he leaned back to look at her breasts snuggled inside a pretty lace bra. Hardened nipples poked at the material as if seeking freedom. And he intended to grant their request.

"Baby, you're beautiful. God! Such soft skin." Hands trembling with need, he searched and released the back snap and then gathered the soft mounds tenderly.

His lips began loving her, his tongue licking, his lips kissing until her squirming made him remember the rest of her writhing body.

Arcing upward, Belle thrust her sensitive, pulsating body against the hardness in his jeans, and Jesse couldn't stop from grinding downward. Belle's moans of joy in this ploy convinced him she wanted more, a lot more. How a guy was supposed to prove his worth as a considerate lover in these circumstances, he couldn't fathom. Going slow was killing him and obviously not what Belle wanted either.

He snaked his hand toward her jeans, undid them, and eased his way inside. Holy hell! The woman was soaking wet. Fantastically dripping wet! Hot and drenched and ready.

# Chapter 25

Belle loved that Jesse took his time for foreplay. Regrettably, in her estimation, he'd worked his way up to *six*–play by now, and she couldn't stand it much longer.

Over two years had passed since she'd been in a man's arms, kissed and caressed, and her ravenous body wanted none of the gentle loving that Jesse so reverently showered her with.

Healthy and very needy, she wanted it hard and fast. The orgasm that hovered just on the brink, close but not quite, was one she was quite frantic to reach.

Since he'd taken her further in her chance to attain a real climax than she'd ever been before, it was desperation that drove her on to be bold.

Gasping, breath choppy, interwoven with whimpers and moans, she begged, "Please Jesse. Now! Please!"

As if he heard the plea, he reached for her wetness

and drove his finger inside. Her body enfolded the intruder lovingly and the crest inched even closer.

Now totally frantic, she pushed against him so she had sufficient room to remove her jeans and was exultant to see him doing the same. He seemed to have greater difficulty so she finished first and lay back to watch the big man disrobe clumsily, endearingly clumsy.

In his haste, he'd gotten his jeans twisted and had some difficulty straightening them. Hearing his sighs of disgust made her grin and feel delight that he wanted her so badly that he couldn't control his frenzy while stripping off his clothes.

A chuckle must have broken loose because when he stood naked before her, his incredible male physique aroused, he shook his head teasingly and said, "You think it's funny that I can barely stand or think coherently for wanting to be inside you?"

*Oh my lord!* Belle melted. "Come here, babe." Her arms rose invitingly. She wanted him buried so deep that she could finally wave goodbye to the loneliness that had been her constant companion for far too long.

Breathless, she welcomed him back, consumed by the emotions he'd built so passionately. His kisses were the means by which to taste him, to feel his need. As he drew her breath from her body using the seduction of his lips she gave up all sense of restraint.

Straddling her, he entered slowly at first. Then he moved with increasing fervor. She wrapped her legs around him and held on for the ride. Sweet pulsations began to form, threatening release. Stronger and stronger until she became so aroused that the sweat poured from her skin. Stimulated beyond bearing, she whimpered.

Unable to stop herself, Belle urged Jesse on and he followed her lead at once, his groan of contentment proof that he loved the way she moved.

All the while he thrust into her willing body, his hands held her face. His mouth traveled from her cheeks to her lips and then to the sweet spot on her neck that guaranteed a reaction.

As if he couldn't help himself, he shifted to stare deep into her eyes. Without a doubt, she knew he could see into her hungry soul. For the first time in her life, she left the way open and let another in.

Belle reached her release first and the contractions of her body ensured that Jesse didn't last much longer before he pulsated with satisfaction also.

Her sighing moans of pleasure were lost in Jesse's groan of delight. His body mashed against hers one last time and then he lowered himself over her and muttered words that made her smile happily—words she'd never forget.

"Sweet Jesus. That was the best."

# Chapter 26

The night passed in cuddles, laughter, another round of lovemaking, and finally sleep. When Belle woke early to realize Jesse still held her tightly, she wiggled her way from the warmth of his arms and crept to her own room. After slipping on her pajama shorts and short t-shirt, she crawled in next to a still sleeping Yaya.

Wide awake now, she recalled the night before. Details flooded, bringing with them an aching need to go back to Jesse and let him appease her returning desire.

Smiling, she had no doubt he'd be more than happy to look after her predicament. The man had an insatiable appetite that delighted her. Tingles flared in her stomach. Without thinking, she rubbed the soft skin and thought of how much it had delighted him when his calloused carpenter hands had stroked her so gently.

"Mommy, I'm *hungwy*." Yaya had her timing down

perfectly.

"So am I, little girl. So am I." When Belle giggled, Yaya crawled over her so that she lay on top like a warm wriggly blanket. Holding both Belle's cheeks in her tiny hands, she kissed Belle good morning and then nestled her face under her mother's neck.

"Mama, do we have-ta go back home today? I'll weally miss Jesse."

"I think we should, button, but why don't we have our breakfast first and make our decision later? We'll see what Jesse has to say. Okay?"

Tumbling off her mother in a hurry to get to her hero, Yaya yelled, "Goodie! I can stay, Jesse."

"Hold it, young lady. That's not what Mama said. Get back here. We have to wash and brush before we go running around."

Chastised but not defeated, Yaya bounced through her morning preparations and scooted out into the kitchen ahead of Belle.

For some reason shyness descended, clinging to her like a tampered-with spiders web.

She made the bed, fiddled in the room, and redid her makeup to match the blouse she changed twice. Finally, fluffing her hair and swallowing her reserve, she made her way down the hall to the open doorway of the kitchen. She watched Jesse who had Yaya giggling and counting her colored cheerios, a game he'd instigated, and that she loved to play.

As if he sensed her there, Jesse looked up and his smile widened. Soft lustful glints shot sparks through the grey eyes that lured her to him, enticing her to walk into the arms he'd opened.

She sent him a loving smile and gave her head a slight shake, sending him a message that all lovers instinctively understand. *Not yet. Let's play this slow.*

Chagrined, his smile fading slightly, he rubbed his hands over his thighs, sat down, and then leaned his elbows on the table. "Good morning, Belle." His words were innocent, but Holy Hell, his tone sent shivers zipping all over her body while her breasts instantly stood to attention. The big jerk knew exactly what he did to her; his delighted grin was proof enough.

Adding a pronounced wiggle to her stride, she entered, smiled her adoration, and when he shifted in his chair and covered his groin, she experienced a wave of delight. *Aha! Two can play the same game.*

Layla, obviously sensing the adults' attention had wandered away from her, broke into the silence. "Mama, what are we going to do today?"

Turning away from the temptation to go over and plunk herself down on Jesse's knee, Belle retrieved her fruit salad and some yogurt from the fridge and joined them. Once she'd sat down, Jesse's hand reached for hers under the table and the world promptly became wonderful.

The big guy waited for her to speak, an invitation in his eyes that she couldn't ignore. "I think Jesse wants us to spend the day with him."

When Yaya let out a shout of approval, Belle interrupted, "But first, we must go home. I haven't checked my e-mails for some time and there could be messages. Then I need to wash some clothes and tidy the place. Once we have our chores finished, we can play. Okay?"

Jesse hesitated before he agreed and Belle knew something was coming. Something she'd have to deal with carefully.

First, he cleared his throat and then he spoke, his voice gentle. "I have to go and pick up my cell phone at Phil's office and I wondered if I might take Layla with me for the ride. It'll give you time alone to get the work done that you want to do."

Okay, now this was a big deal. Could Belle let Yaya out of her sight so soon? Should she?

Yaya clapped her hands, gleefully adding, "Mama. Can I go with Jesse? Please? I'll be a *good* girl."

Belle looked from one begging face to the other. Yaya's lit with innocence. Jesse, not too stupid, knew her struggle. He'd asked for her trust and they both knew if they were to have a future it was a line that eventually needed to be crossed.

Taking her time, she realized that the thought of Jesse looking after her most precious beloved didn't frighten her. Since her baby had been snatched from under her very nose, a horrible bubble of fear and distrust had begun to form inside like a cancerous growth. But picturing her baby with this man made it dissipate. It would be fine. She trusted him.

"Sure. Yaya would love to go with you."

# Chapter 27

Sometime later, driving with Layla firmly ensconced in the truck's back seat in her car seat, Jesse enjoyed her performance. The little munchkin only knew a few lines of a nursery rhyme, and so she sang it over and over.

Once again, he checked the rear-view mirror and watched her for a second as she held her baby doll in her arms, rocked it back and forth, and serenaded.

While she kept herself amused, he revisited the important conversation with Belle that had allowed Layla to be with him this morning. When he'd asked permission to bring her with him, he'd known it would be a test.

The day before, shopping at the mall and taking in the movie, not for one second had Belle let Layla out of her sight. She'd either held her in her arms or they'd clasped hands. Once, when the little girl had stepped away to get Jesse's attention, agitated, Belle had raised her voice to chastise her. "Don't let go of

Mommy. You have to hold my hand all the time."

Being a happy little soul, Layla shrugged and said, "Sowwy, Mama. I'll be careful."

Mollified, Belle had seen him watching and she'd sent him an apologetic look. He'd smiled at her, knowing her fear had nothing to do with him and everything to do with the nightmare she'd suffered the day before. One thing he'd figured out by her behavior, if they were to have any kind of a relationship, Jesse had to know she trusted him with Layla.

When it came time for her to sneak away and get Layla's baby doll, he could see the anxious way she acted. Finally, he offered to get the present and hide it in the truck then meet the other two in front of the movie in twenty minutes. Passing over sufficient money, she'd blessed him with her eyes and smiled her relief.

The singing from the back had stopped and the sudden silence caught his attention. Once again he checked the rear-view and he cleared his throat softly, rather than letting the hovering laugh erupt.

Stopped at a red light, the vehicle next to him had a small boy sitting by the back-door window closest to his truck. The shenanigans of the two children, keeping themselves amused, delighted him. In the naughty way of kids everywhere, Layla, tired of serenading, was now making faces at the kid in the car next to them. Sure enough, Jesse could just make out the grinning boy's cheeky tongue sticking out also.

If his heart hadn't already opened a special niche for this precious kid, he knew that every minute they spent together she was becoming far too important. As it was, he couldn't imagine her not being a part of his life—her and her mother.

"Jesse, can we buy my mommy a Christmas pwesent? Like we talked about yesterday?"

"Sure, sweetheart. I've asked my friend, Phil, to bring my phone outside to the car so we won't have to get out or find a parking spot. Then we can go to a store and you can find your mom something nice, okay?"

"Okay! How come Mr. Phil has your phone?"

"I dropped it yesterday at your uncle's place when I went to pick you up."

"Oh." The silence lengthened and Jesse thought she'd been satisfied. He should have known the little chatterbox had more to say. "Is Uncle Jack sick, Jesse?"

"What makes you ask that? Did he act sick when you were with him?"

"He cwied when I said I wanted to go home to you and Mommy. I felt sowwy for him so I told him I'd stay with him a bit longer."

"Did he scare you?"

Again, she took her time to answer. Finally, in a timid voice, she said, "No. He didn't scare me. He looks like my daddy's picture. So I knew he liked me."

"Of course, he likes you. We all like you even if you are a bwat."

Layla's delighted giggles made him laugh also. When they spotted Phil in his chair waiting by the curb, Jesse pulled over and rolled down the window to reach for his cell. "Thanks for bringing it out here. How's everything?" His warning nod toward the back seat made Phil aware there were little ears and big eyes paying rapt attention.

"No problem, I was on my way out anyway. Things are swell. Couldn't be better! Have a new recruit for our program and he's taking to it well. Duck to water. Figure the medication the doctor prescribed has helped him tremendously. He'll be good for day trips soon. Might want to consider it with the holidays close and all."

"I'll keep that in mind."

# Chapter 28

As soon as the other two left, Belle gathered her dirty laundry and high-tailed it over to her place where she could put in a load before doing anything else.

As soon as she stepped into her small front room, much smaller than Kim's spacious place, she missed the decorations, the lights, and the presence of Sam.

From the time she'd moved in, the little monster had decided she needed a guard and so he followed her everywhere. When the furry baby saw her leaving, he'd whined piteously, jumping up and begging to come with her, but she knew she wouldn't get anything done. The temptation to play with the little beggar wasn't easily ignored.

Whipping around getting her chores crossed off the mental list, weariness struck and convinced her to make a cup of tea and take a break.

Her computer lured her and soon she was guiltily checking her banking, writing e-mails, and catching up on Facebook. A chat message opened up and Kim typed in that she would Skype in a few minutes if Belle were up for a visit.

Happily, she acquiesced and soon the two girls were yakking. "Where's Yaya?" Kim's eyes had searched behind Belle for the child that was always allowed to say hello before Belle sent her to play so they could have privacy.

"She's with Jesse. He had a chore to do and thought she might like to go for a ride. I suspect he's taking her shopping to buy her Christmas presents."

Kim's surprise faded to gladness. "How do you know she's going shopping?"

"Once they were ready to leave, she asked me for her 'lowance. Could I give her two whole dollars? When I asked her why she wanted money, she said she couldn't tell me 'cause then I'd know she was buying me a *pwesent*."

Delighted with the typical Yaya story, Kim laughed and said, "She's so precious, Belle. You're so lucky."

"Oh, I know." In few words, Belle explained to Kim about the nightmare she'd lived through two days before.

"I'm glad you moved in with Jesse. I would have made you come if I'd have been there myself."

"I knew you wouldn't mind. Just the thought of

staying alone in the apartment where I knew Jack could return scared me silly. And then, as if his visits weren't bad enough, to have him take Yaya away without asking permission drove me insane."

While Belle told the story of the abduction, she watched Kim's eyes grow larger. Her expressive face underwent continuous changes from horror to anger and then relief. In the end, she said, "You'll never have to worry about Jesse. He loves kids. I couldn't have asked for a better brother."

Delight filled Belle as she listened to Kim talk about the man she herself adored. Tingles spread throughout her body, from her chest to her tummy until her hands unconsciously reached to massage.

Kim, catching the movement, changed the subject. "Is your stomach bothering you again?"

"Not near as bad as before. Ever since Jesse figured out that I most likely had an intolerance to gluten, I've stayed away from all foods with flour and it's been like a miracle. He went ahead and organized a doctor's appointment at the same place his friend's mother goes who has the same problem. Once there, I'll get a proper diagnosis."

Kim's grin spread, highlighting her dimples and bringing a sparkle to her beautiful green eyes. "You have a crush on my brother, dontcha?"

Belle swept her hands up to cover her face. As

soon as she realized how telling her actions, she pretended to sweep them through her hair but she was too late.

"Sweet! You're involved! My friend, I can see it written all over your pretty face. Every time you say his name, it's like a worshipper uttering the name of some godlike creature."

Belle laughed. "Jesus, I'm not that bad." Then she thought for a moment and added, "Am I?"

Amused, Kim replied, "Oh yeah, my friend, you've got it bad. And I couldn't be happier. It's been hell watching my crazy brother carrying his broken heart around all these years. His childhood romance should have ended when Mari left, but once Jesse makes up his mind that he cares, the man's a lifer."

"Then I'm a very lucky woman."

The phone near Belle's elbow rang and startled both girls.

"Gotta go. It might be Jesse."

"And I can see how much that thought disturbs you. Your eyes just lit up and the smile you're wearing is disgracefully happy. Okay, I'll let you go. Bye now." Kim rang off; her laughter hanging in the air even after her face disappeared.

Belle casually leaned back in her chair, picked up the receiver, and said a sweet hello.

# Chapter 29

"Belle, this is your stepsister, Marilyn Dangerfield. I know we've never met but your father asked me to call."

"Is everything all right?" Belle jerked forward and leaned her head on her hand. Anxiety grabbed at her guts and if her premonition proved to be correct, she knew the news would be bad.

"Not really. My mother passed away recently, leaving your father a widower. He's very lonely, so he's made up his mind that he wants to reach out and make amends with your side of the family before it's too late."

"What do you mean, too late?"

"Mother was ill for a long time and your father was her primary caregiver. I believe that her death has prompted this decision not to let any more time pass before he reaches out."

Still not sure where the conversation was leading, Belle spoke with utter truth. "I'm very sorry for your loss. But I still don't understand. Is Dad ill?"

"Thank you. No he's not really ill, just sick at heart."

Belle listened to the words and felt her soft heart lurch.

"Why I called is to ask a favor of you. I wonder if we can possibly intrude on you for a few days. We're arriving in the Seattle area tomorrow, and if at all possible, father's wish is to visit with you and your family."

"You'd like to stay *here*... with me?"

"If you don't have room, either we can both take a hotel or I can. It's just that he knows you have a child and is hopeful that you'll let him stay so he can get to know her."

"How did he find out about Yaya?"

"Yaya? I thought her name was Layla?"

"Yes it is. Yaya's only her nickname."

"And one I'm sure you're hoping she'll grow out of soon." A polite chuckle followed but it didn't make Belle feel like joining in.

"How did you find us? We've moved recently."

"I'm a lawyer, dear, with a lot of friends in law enforcement. It wasn't hard."

A niggling dismay caught hold and she shook it off. She was just being picky and not like herself. Time to grow up and accept the hand of friendship her father and stepsister were extending.

For most of her life, Belle had lived alone, she truly believed that strong family support was precious and to be welcomed and appreciated. When her friends had invited her to various family-type functions, a small part of her yearned to be like them, to have someone who cared because you belonged. "I'd love to see you both. You're traveling with him?"

"Yes. I recently filed for a divorce and needed a break from my law practice in L.A. Father surprised me with a visit and we're planning on traveling over the holidays. It's a lonely time for folks without any family. When he arrived, I knew something was eating away at him. Once he explained, I decided to start the ball rolling and call you."

"I'm glad you did, Marilyn. *Really!* It's fine for you both to come and stay in my apartment. For the last few days, I've been living with a friend down the hall. He'd be more than happy for Layla and me to stay longer. Therefore, you and father could have my apartment to yourselves and only be two doors away from us. Do you need the address?"

"Got it. And Belle, that would be just perfect! We'll only stay the one day and be out of your way by Christmas Eve."

"Nonsense. Why not plan to stay for the holiday? I know Layla would be thrilled to have more people around to spoil her."

"Wonderful. I'll let Father know and I'll send you a text when to expect our arrival tomorrow."

"Can't wait to meet you and catch up with Dad. Bye for now."

As soon as Belle knew the connection had been broken, she ran to get the old photo album from the hall closet. Before she'd taken off, her mother had passed it to her saying, "I have no use for these old pictures. I've taken the few I want. You can either keep the rest or throw them away for all I care."

Of course, Belle had kept them. Moved them with her from place to place and not once had she opened the book until now.

The happiness whizzing around inside her all day clouded over for a few seconds until she had a little talk with herself. *Oh, grow up! These pictures and the memories they hold can't hurt you unless you let them.*

The first few were of an immature couple obviously in love. Her mother looked as if she adored the young, good-looker who appeared charming if his huge smile was any indication.

The next few showed the early baby pictures where Belle seemed to be the apple of her dad's eye. In fact, every photo showed her with him, being rocked in his arms or carried on his shoulders as if he were proud of the cute baby he'd produced.

There were none of her mother holding her, and very few where they were together in the same frame. A chill worked its way into Belle's heart. She closed her eyes to go back to a place in time she hated to remember.

Scenes played in her head and she saw again the mean-tempered woman who never let up on either her industrious husband or a daughter who tried as hard as she knew how to please a mother who hated the role.

Belle remembered that, in the beginning, the battles had mostly been about her mother's behavior toward Belle. The woman's quick temper and how it incited a lot of nasty lickings. Then the fights spiraled to include money, the dump they had to live in, and even his inability to satisfy her in bed.

Her mother's laziness had been another issue. Belle knew it had been her father and herself who'd kept the house as best they could for a woman who kept losing jobs until she gave up trying.

Vaguely, she recalled the final breakup. Already, at seventeen, she'd moved from the house to stay with a friend who lived closer to one of the jobs Belle had found at a fast-food joint.

The night in question, Belle had returned to get the rest of her things only to hear them going at it yet again. This time, she'd stood outside the door and listened. Her mother's ranting swelled over her father's attempt to calm her. "You never loved me. Admit it! All you ever cared about was Belle. The stinking kid got more attention from you than I ever did."

"So, what kind of a woman does that make you? Jealous of your own baby. From the day she was born, you've let my love for her eat away at you until I had to pretend she meant nothing just to keep the peace. You turned me into a disgusting father and for what? You never forgave me for getting you pregnant anyway. Now she can't stand the sight of either of us. I'm through! Even though I'll never forgive myself, I just hope one day my baby will forgive me for being such a weakling."

Arms wrapped around her stomach, vision blurred, Belle left. Her mother called her a few months later to tell her to get her ass over there and get her stuff. That's when she heard about her father moving away with another woman and her mother's plans to move up north.

The hammering beat of her heart returned her to the present where she sat stiffened from the remembered agony. Surprised to see tears dripping, Belle shook herself out of the past. Her clenched hands had crumpled the last page of the album, so she tried to smooth it out. A vicious headache, circling her head like a band of dread, seized her and reminded her once again of why she didn't like to think about her childhood.

Her father had been right in his assessment of how she'd felt about him. As much as she'd disliked her mother, she'd blamed him in the end. She'd relied on him and he'd never put a stop to the situation. As a young girl, she'd prayed for him to take her with him and just leave. Instead, he'd chosen to do so with a new family.

Now that same man was returning to her world. A place where she'd worked so hard to provide sun instead of clouds and storms.

Laughter instead of screams and threats.

Love instead of fear and weakness.

Could she really let her father inside this protective bubble she'd built around her and Yaya?

Him... or Jesse?

# Chapter 30

Yaya burst through the door, her cheeks pink and her eyes full of glee. "Mama, I bought you a pwesent for Christmas. It's a..."

Jesse laughingly cupped her mouth with a gentle hand, shook his head, and said, "Uh-huh."

Giggling merrily, Yaya put her hands over his and nodded. Once free, she continued as if he'd never stopped her. "...surprise."

Their simple cheer dissipated all Belles' earlier trepidation, just like when the warmth from a fire clears away the room's cold.

Happy once again, Belle joined in their fun. "A surprise? Now I can't wait for Christmas morning so I can see what it is."

"Jesse got you a surprise too. A little one, right Jesse? It's in a small box so it's vewy little."

Belle's eyes flew to Jesse's face where he tried his damnedest to look innocent. "We had an understanding, presents for k-i-d-s only." She shook her finger teasingly.

"You said it. I never agreed. Look, I don't expect anything in return. Let me play Santa this year, please. It matters to me, Belle." He moved in her direction, a definite goal in mind. Her heart swelled to see hunger mixed with what one could only call adoration spread over his face.

Her hands flew out to stop his forward momentum and ended up circling his cheeks when he bent his head to put his lips on hers.

Yaya's giggling tore them apart and ended their goal of finding relief from the increasing need to touch and hold.

Sam had decided that Yaya's pant legs needed straightening and the enthusiastic little beast had her hem between his teeth, pulling back and forth. Giving way, Yaya finally fell in a heap of chortles and pushed at him to make him stop. The pup, knowing a playmate when he found one, pounced on her tummy and tried washing her face.

Both Belle and Jesse ran to her rescue. Jesse picked up the over-excited mutt while Belle scooped up Yaya and stood her so she could help her take off her outer clothes.

"I have some very good news to share." As Belle spoke the words, an odd shiver worked its way up her back to the nape of her neck, working hard to get all those neck hairs to stand at attention. She shook off the feeling and continued. "My father and stepsister will be arriving tomorrow and would like to join us for Christmas."

Yaya stopped moving and looked up at her mom. Her green eyes held a surprisingly keen look as she stared at Belle to gauge her acceptance.

Belle smiled, making sure her eyes showed only delight at the news. "It'll be lovely to see him again and finally meet her."

"Are they my family too, Mommy?"

"Yes. My father is your grandfather and my stepsister will be an aunt."

"Like Auntie Kim?"

"Kind of." Belle heard Jesse chuckle and knew he was getting a kick out of her predicament.

Happy again, Yaya ran to Jesse who'd finished putting his gift, wrapped in golden paper with a bow to match, on a higher branch of the tree where the sharp-toothed canine who loved to chew couldn't get at it.

She reached up her arms, taking for granted that he'd want to pick her up. Jesse didn't disappoint. "I have another auntie and a gwampa, Jesse. I'm a very lucky girl, right?" She laid her head on his shoulder as if seeking his protection from these unknown strangers.

"You sure are, sunshine." He glanced toward Belle, his eyes shining with what one could only call elation. "I suggest that if you're having all this company, you and your mom will have to stay here with me so they will have enough room at your apartment."

Belle grinned at the way he looked at her yet used Yaya as his prompter. She never let him down either.

"Yay! Mommy, Jesse wants us to stay with him and Sam and Puff and Snowball and—"

Belle stopped her before she named all the fish in the tank. "Yes, honey. I know. I'm glad he wants us because I did tell Marilyn that they could stay at my apartment knowing we'd be fine here."

He stepped close to Belle, put his arm around her shoulder, and squeezed. "That's settled then. I guess we'd better grab a bite of lunch and then we'll all go shopping at the supermarket for some groceries. Looks like we'll have to buy us a large turkey-bird for the big day!"

# Chapter 31

By the time they returned from shopping and Jesse put the groceries away, Belle had changed the sheets on both the beds back in her apartment.

Earlier, she'd worked darn hard to get the place spic and span. Most of her furniture had come from garage sales and online ads but she had chosen wisely, making every penny count by selecting quality over fashion.

Therefore, her place wasn't the latest in style but it was surprisingly classy. Her good taste had added in the froufrou where it needed to perk up the placid colors. Her flair made the older-fashioned rooms surprisingly cozy. Not up to the standards of Kim's place where Jesse had worked wonders, but since she rented and didn't own, it wasn't a dump—and for that she was glad.

Standing to survey the beige corduroy sofa, chaise lounge and chair highlighted with the red faux-suede pillows, she noticed how her big fern by her window showed up so well and the silver-framed pictures of Yaya stood out on the mantle.

Crossing her arms, Belle sighed. Nothing was going to make her feel ashamed, not the fact that she didn't have a job at the moment or that she was living with a man who wasn't Yaya's father. She certainly didn't need to try and "put on the dog" when she had no doubt her lawyer stepsister would be much higher up the financial ladder. Still, she wanted to be at her best.

After all, she had her pride. Once she'd left behind the life that had dragged her through the heartache of self-hate, she'd crawled out of the morass of pity and learned the lesson of self-worth—that it mattered more what she thought than anyone else.

She'd worked desperately to love herself, to be honest with herself, and to take pride in herself. It hadn't been easy but she'd done it by reading a lot of self-help books and then applying the rules.

Straightening her shoulders, Belle gathered the paper from the huge poinsettia plant she'd bought as a final decoration and now adorned the table, turned on the Christmas lights to the small tree by the window, and turned to greet Jesse and Yaya who just walked in the front door.

Jesse touched her back, the heat from his hand scorching skin sensitive to his touch. Unable to stop herself, she leaned into him and loved that he braced her and even encircled her waist. "Belle, it looks very nice."

"Mama, you put the Christmas tree up. Can I look for my special ownaments?"

"Sure, honey. I put them low so you could find them. I figured your grandfather and Auntie Marilyn would like to have a tree for themselves. They can share ours at Jesse's place but it'll be nice for them to have one here also."

Jesse whispered close to her ear. "You're nervous! Why?"

Yaya moved out of range and Belle answered, her voice lowered. "They're like strangers to me, Jesse. I'll tell you more later."

His arm tightened possessively and she thought her knees would give way when his hardness pressed against her, informing her of how affected he was by her nearness. He kissed her ear before uttering words that delighted her. "In bed?"

# Chapter 32

As soon as Jesse had finished reading Layla her second story, purposefully making his voice low and mesmerizing, hoping to make her sleepy, she dropped off. Her hand fell away from his arm where she'd held on to him all the while as if fearing that he would leave before she was ready to let him go.

He gazed down and saw long eyelashes sweeping her sleep-flushed cheeks, hair that a little girl had chopped to different lengths to get it out of her eyes, and a bow-like mouth with a slight smile hovering at the corner as if her dreams were pleasant.

"Is she sleeping?" Belle stood at the open doorway, a smile lighting her eyes that flustered him.

"She fought it through the first book and had to give in by halfway into the second. She's a trooper though." He grinned, surprised by how incredibly happy he felt.

"I'll have to even her hair out tomorrow, I guess. I left it so that it would grow back before trimming.

I hate to cut it 'cause it kind of suits her, the shaggy look."

"I wouldn't change a thing. It's endearing and cute. Chances are it'll never happen again so we'll have to take more pictures for keepsakes."

"The little actress loves getting her photo taken, as you well know already since your phone has been busy for days. I never knew men liked to take so many... ahhh, keepsakes?"

Belle's teasing never failed to disarm him. The craving he'd fought all day sprung up. He wanted to hold her and preferably while in his bed. The unrelenting ache to have her close was becoming unbearable. Jesse guided her into the hallway and closed the door to Kim's bedroom.

Then he turned toward her, his arms lifting, hands reaching. When she stepped inside the haven, he blessed the saints and every God in the universe that he'd found the love of his life. Take it slow. Don't scare her. Teach her about how you love completely and give her time to learn.

First, he kissed her, and when her sweet response devastated, he whispered, his voice rough with emotion, "I want you in my bed tonight, Belle. Will you come?"

"Will you make it worth my while?"

Laughing, Jesse swung her over his shoulder,

lightly smacked her behind, and headed toward his room. "Oh, baby. You're gonna have to learn that teasing a hungry man is dangerous."

# Chapter 33

Early the next day, Belle thought about the wonder of the night before when Jesse had loved her so sweetly, lifting her to peaks she never knew possible. They'd hungrily explored each other's bodies with kisses and strokes, while moans of ecstasy and encouraging love phrases reverberated around the room. In the end, she'd ridden him (a first for her) and the power of being in control had been an exquisite experience. Sweet, yet at the same time seductive, it had lifted her passion to new heights.

A number of times, she'd even felt that Jesse had been on the verge of declaring his love. At one point, he'd stared into her eyes and whispered, "forever."

The smell of burning bacon brought her back to earth and the smoke-filled kitchen. Making breakfast while Jesse and Yaya took Sam outside for a walk, Belle had to stop daydreaming about their future and think about now and what the heck she was doing to their breakfast. She threw the

overcooked meat into a dish to cool and added more
to the sizzling pan.

Since she knew Jesse had a fondness for a full
breakfast, she had decided to cook one for him. In
fact, she'd do almost anything to please him today.
She wanted that man—as a husband for her and a
father for Yaya, Jesse was perfect.

If he wanted to woo her, take his time, that would
be fine with her but he wasn't getting away, not with
her heart.

Belle reflected that should Jesse decide he really
did want to step up their relationship, she had to be
in a good place, centered and healthy. Therefore, she
had to make some changes.

It was more than time to get her life back on track.
She made a note to call her old boss later and let
her know she'd be ready to return to work after the
holidays. Thankfully, Yaya came to work with her at
the daycare and so they spent more time together.
Although her baby joined in the fun with the other
kids and the various activities, she had a habit of
constantly combing the room for sight of her mom.

Seeing as how there was no daddy in the picture,
at least for now, Belle guessed that was normal for
a child of a single parent. Even though she'd made
up her mind not to dwell on the past, thoughts of
her family's pending visit snuck in and wouldn't be

dislodged. After sharing some of her reserves last night with Jesse, he'd helped her decide that she shouldn't overthink anything but take things as they came.

The door opened and Yaya flew toward her, the pompom on her sweater bouncing with every skipping step. "Mama, can we still make cookies for Gwampa today?"

Belle watched as Jesse approached and sent her a wink. He wiped Sam's feet and lowered the wriggling bundle so the pup could bound in her direction and shower her with his own leaping style of "hi-I'm-home-aren't-you-glad?" kind of adoration.

"Sure, muffin, we'll make cookies and perogies and bread. Then we'll be ready for company. Go and hang your sweater on the chair, wash your hands and come get breakfast. Then we'll start."

"Okay!" Both puppy and child ran to the hallway, having to leap over the two Persian princesses who blocked their way.

Jesse stood still, hands on hips and a delighted grin lighting his face. "Seriously? You make perogies? And bread? I think I've died and gone to heaven."

"Yes, seriously. I have a Polish friend who loves to share her cooking skills. I can promise you that

Christmas dinner will be a meal fit for a king."

Jesse prowled behind her and whispered so only she could hear, "I've been in the kingdom of heaven ever since I met you. Does that make me a king?"

Man the guy knew how to weaken her knees! A quick kiss that turned into a lustful tease soon got interrupted when bouncing feet were heard returning.

As the day started, so it continued. Hungry glances interrupted by a beaming happy child while everyone had jobs to do getting the place ready for their expected company.

Finally, while the baking ham filled the room with glorious smells and the last of the decorations were added to the cookies, a text message appeared saying their guests had arrived.

"I'll go and show them my apartment and let them get settled, and then I'll bring them here to you and Yaya. That okay?"

"Absolutely. Yaya and I will put some of those cookies on a platter while you're gone. Right, Layla?"

"Wight, Jesse." Seeing the devil in his eye, and the cheeky grin on her daughter's face, she warned them both. "Only one each or you'll spoil your dinner."

Rather than use the elevator, Belle ran down the stairs and got there in time to help an older version of her father with his bag. "Hello, Belle. You look wonderful... happy. I'm glad."

Belle searched his face, seeing the pain and age embedded into the wrinkles he'd grown since she'd last seen him. He'd dressed in a suit for the occasion and his mustache was neatly trimmed along with the thinning grey hair. "Hello, Dad." She smiled and hugged his portly body, hearing his sigh of relief as he held her close and patted her back over and over.

A beautiful woman who'd finished paying the driver stepped toward her, smiled kindly, and held out her hand. "I'm Marilyn Dangerfield, your stepsister. Thank you, Belle, for inviting us for the holiday."

Belle shook the proffered hand and searched the face of a stunning woman. Styled by a pro, Marilyn's blonde hair had been pinned in the back leaving her features prominent and breathtaking. Green eyes, similar to her own, were surveying her at the same time and seemed to like what they saw since the small polite smile now reached her eyes and lit them into a sparkling wonder.

"You're very welcome," Belle said. "I'm happy to finally meet you. Come with me. First I'll show you where you'll be staying and then we can go to the apartment two doors down where I have supper ready and waiting. You must be starving?"

Her father answered with a chuckle, "I'm starving to meet my granddaughter. Is she here?"

"She's waiting for you upstairs."

"Then let's hurry. You won't take too long will you, Marilyn?"

She laughed and answered, "We'll go straight there, Dad." She turned to Belle and said, "He's been fussing about Layla all day. We can just drop the things off and then meet Layla if you don't mind."

In no time at all, Belle pointed her father in the direction of Layla's room and led Marilyn into her own space. Through the other woman's eyes, her haven suddenly seemed dowdy and cheap, which annoyed Belle. She had no right to believe her sister so shallow—until she heard the cool tone in the polite words. "It's fine... and comfortable. Thank you."

Then her doubt re-emerged.

Her father hovered in the doorway. "Can we go now to visit with Layla? I have a special gift for her." He carried a small, Christmas-wrapped parcel sporting a red satin bow.

Belle smiled and led the way. "You should give it to her for Christmas."

"Oh, I have another one for Christmas. This one is different and I want her to have it now."

Belle opened Kim's apartment door, happy that

at least this classy room shone with beauty and a perfect feeling of Christmas. Most important of all, the two people who she loved more than anything else in the world were there waiting to be showed off and shared.

Layla suddenly shy, hugged onto Jesse's leg while hiding her face. He patted her back before looking up. Then he took a halting step forward as he breathed one word that tore Belle's happiness into tiny unbearable shards.

"Mari!"

# Chapter 34

Belle froze. Her nerves rioted as she hugged herself and rocked in place like she did when she soothed her baby.

Desperately, she tried to control the waves of emotion from becoming wails of denial. Biting her bottom lip, she blinked more than once so she could see through the gathering tears. Deep breathing helped somewhat until Marilyn flew across the space and flung herself into Jesse's open arms. Then Belle knew she either had to leave the room or make a complete fool out of herself.

She backed away, snuck around the furniture, and fled into the kitchen. I can't take it! Oh, God! Not now... Her hands covered her face while images of Jesse holding another woman flooded into her mind and took root.

Small hands pulled at her for attention. Obviously, Yaya had followed her rather than staying with strangers. "Mommy, Gwampa is here.

We have to meet him."

Belle reached for a tissue from a nearby box and used it to mop up before turning to smile at her daughter's uneasiness. "Yes, baby. Mommy forgot something on the stove. It's fine now. Let's go and introduce you."

Squaring her shoulders, Belle lifted Yaya as a shield and returned to the room in time to see that Jesse had now put space between himself and Marilyn. In fact, he was in the midst of offering refreshments as they'd planned for him to do earlier. He seemed rather relieved when she appeared and although she sensed his drawing gaze, she ignored him. Instead, she moved toward the older man who rose as soon as she came close.

"Father, I'd like you to meet my little ray of sunshine, Layla Foster. And Layla, this is your Grampa Harry. Say hello like I showed you."

"Hello." Layla held her tiny hand out in front of her and waited for Belle's father to shake. He didn't disappoint. "How do you do, Miss Foster? May I call you Layla?"

"O-kay. Can I call you Gwampa?"

The older man beamed with approval and grinned, his tidy grey mustache framing his lips. "Of course, sweetheart! I have a special present for you. Would you like to open it?"

"Yes please." Layla wriggled from her mother's reluctant arms so she could go to where her grampa pointed at a small, beautifully wrapped gift. Lost without something to cling to, Belle knelt to watch Yaya opening her surprise.

In the meantime, Marilyn carried on with explanations. "Dad, Jesse is a really old friend of mine. In fact, we were childhood sweethearts in high school. I believe I've told you about him. We spent every moment together during the final year, before Mom and I moved with you to L.A."

"Yes. I remember how you mooned over his picture until you got all wrapped up in going to college and met Steve."

Marilyn shot Harry a warning look and then smiled once again at Jesse.

Eavesdropping, Belle saw her father's frown when he noticed the proprietary way that Marilyn held on to Jesse's arm. Belle sensed that he didn't like this unexpected situation any better than she did and was relieved by the fact.

Being a gentleman, he smiled politely as he accepted the glass of wine his host provided. Then he quickly stepped back to watch Layla's face when she saw what he had brought for her.

Snug in a pink velvet jewelry box, one Belle vaguely remembered, was a dainty gold ring with a tiny heart in the center. In the same parcel was a small ornately framed photograph of a little, golden-haired cherub. She wore the same ring, plus a gigantic smile as she proudly showed her hand to the photographer.

Layla, her green eyes shining with pure delight, clutched the box and swung her gaze to Belle. "Can I wear it, Mama?"

"Of course, sweetheart, but you must never take it off or you might lose it. If for any reason you want to remove it, you bring it to me so I can keep it safe for you. Okay?"

"Yes, Mama. I pwomise." Solemnly, Layla nodded her head and slipped the ring onto her finger. "It's beau-ti-ful. Thank you, Gwampa." Harry nodded, obviously too overcome to speak. He coughed to clear away the emotion. "Do you know who that is in the photograph, Layla?"

"No."

"It's your mommy. She was three and a half, the same age as you, in that picture."

"Oh!" Clearly not understanding the importance of the photo, Layla dropped it back onto the table and with a happy grin, she ran to show Jesse her prize.

Smiling, he picked her up in his arms. "See what Gwampa bought me, Jesse? It's my mama's ring."

"It's very pretty, sunshine. You're a lucky girl." He turned her toward Marilyn who still glowed with the satisfaction of meeting up with an old flame. "Have you met your Auntie Mari yet?"

"I don't have an auntie Mawi." Layla narrowed her eyes and stared first at him and then at the woman standing very close. She crossed her arms and her bottom lip poked out slightly. "My auntie's name is Mawilyn. Mommy said so."

Jesse laughed and agreed. "You're right. This is your Auntie Marilyn. Mari is just a nickname like Yaya. Say hello like a good girl."

Layla leaned her head on his shoulder and peeked at Marilyn who wore an inviting smile.

"I'm very pleased to meet you, Layla. I've been looking forward to it for a long time."

Not one to ignore a pleasant manner, Layla succumbed to the gracious greeting and in a very small voice, she answered, "Hello." Then she wriggled to be released. "I want to show Sam my ring."

Once he'd lowered her, Layla ran to her room where, earlier, they'd shut in the rambunctious puppy.

After she left the room, Belle picked up the picture and surprisingly tumbled back in time. She knew how delighted she'd been when her father had given her the ring. But it hadn't lasted past the Christmas holiday because her mother had taken it away from her.

Her glance flew to her father who watched for her reaction. He knew she'd remembered. He stooped next to her and put his hand on her shoulder. "Do you remember that every time we went out together, you got to wear your ring? Then one day, you just outgrew it?"

Relief washed over her when his happy recollections overrode her ugly ones. "Yes, I remember. We used to go out quite often, didn't we?"

"When you were younger. Then, your mom got worse and every time I'd take you with me, she'd make you pay. Pretty soon, I had to stop."

"Truthfully, Dad, I never knew why you put up with her for as long as you did."

"Oh, that's easy. I stayed because of you. When you were younger, you didn't seem quite so affected by her mean ways. Unfortunately, as the years went by, you changed, became closed in and unreachable. I tried, but you shut me out and I didn't push. I don't blame you for not wanting me either. I let you down in a bad way. I guess you hated me."

"No, not you," replied Belle. "I just hated the life. Living with you both being so unhappy wore me down, I guess. It got so I mostly existed in my own little world. But that's behind us now." Belle desperately wanted to change the subject. How could she explain to this nice man today how, back then, she'd needed him to stand up for her, to fight for her so she'd have felt a sense of worth?

"Mama, can we eat now? I'm hungwy."

Saved by the pangs in a little girl's tummy!

"Sure. It'll take me a few minutes to cook the perogies and then we'll be ready. You can come and help."

Jesse piped up when he heard the words. "I'll help too."

Belle wouldn't look at him. Instead, she took Layla's hand and spoke over her shoulder. "No thank you, Jesse. I'll call when it's ready. Please stay and visit with Dad and Mari."

# Chapter 35

Jesse knew he was in trouble. Shivers of anxiety raced over his body. They ended up clashing in his head where a harsh headache warned he'd be paying soon. He had to get Belle aside and try to smooth the waters... but he didn't quite trust himself to let her look too deeply into his eyes.

Knowing that Belle had heard the sound of wonder and happiness that rang out when he'd said Mari's name, he couldn't lie his way from that truth. Why he'd reacted that way, God only knew. Was there still some leftover passion for the girl who he'd worshipped for so many years? Truly, he didn't think so. His mind traveled back.

When Mari had thrown herself into his arms, she must have thought they were open to welcome her. In actual fact, the action had been a spontaneous move, showing shock. But she'd taken it as an invitation and had responded accordingly with a hug that lasted a few seconds too long to be acceptable. Instinctively, his arms had enclosed her.

While she'd draped herself around him, he'd smelled the perfume she wore and it had changed from the lighter, flowery scent she used to prefer. Now she wore a musky, kinda sexy fragrance that was meant to disturb a man's equilibrium—and did. However, not in a good way! It irritated. Like a pushy woman would irritate a shyer man.

At that moment, he remembered Belle and looked up in time to see her stiff back as she guided Layla in opening her present.

The silence became uncomfortable for Jesse. Purposely, he moved Mari aside and filled the void with small talk. "How weird is this? When you left all those years ago, it was because your mom had married Belle's father."

"Yes. Harry's been my stepdad for the last ten years. Sadly, Mom passed away recently and he's been very lonely. That's the reason for the visit."

"Yeah, Belle told me her father wanted to renew connections and meet his granddaughter. She mentioned a stepsister. I guess since you were living with Harry, I thought you a much older person."

Mari laughed, but without humor. "She might be my little sister but it's only a matter of a couple of years. And I don't live with Harry. I live in my own place. Harry was having some issues with the holidays approaching and I was at a loose end and decided to cheer him up. It's what prompted me to call Belle."

All the while he listened to Mari; Jesse watched Belle and Layla until his little champion flew at him with her hand held out, flaunting a new prized possession.

Loving the happiness shining from her adorable green eyes, Jesse introduced her to Mari and was astonished at the blatant green-eyed monster this small girl-child displayed toward her new aunt.

Layla turned away from Marilyn and gripped Jesse as tightly as she ever had. Her reluctance to admit Mari into the family circle had his macho ego grinning. Hard to imagine that possessive behavior could start in one so young but then again, what the hell did he know about the female psyche?

Once Layla forced him to put her down, something he was reluctant to do since she created an effective barrier, his attention was drawn to Belle and her father. They were huddled together; her hand being held ever so carefully in his wrinkled palm. Important issues about a framed picture were being discussed and Jesse sensed they needed this time.

Decision made, he smiled at Mari and said, "So tell me, what've you been up to over these last years?"

Feigning interest, he listened while keeping an eye on Belle and her expressions. By the time Layla came begging her mom for dinner, Belle seemed more resigned than anything else. Thankfully, Mari had wound down and decided to renew her glass of wine so he went to sit down next to Harry who looked rather forlorn.

Jesse picked up the photograph he believed was the crux of Belle's pain and felt his heart melt into a puddle of pure affection. "It's Belle as a child. She's adorable."

"Yes," Harry said, "She's pretty close to the same age as Layla is today."

"It's amazing. They could be twins." Jesse passed the photo over to Mari whose hand waited.

"I have a picture of myself at that age at home. It's strange how we all look so much alike."

Politely ignoring her self-centeredness, Jesse asked, "I don't think you mentioned it earlier... where's your home now, Mari?"

"I live in L.A. and used to work for Winle, Pawne and Brown, a rather prestigious law firm in the city."

Harry spoke up and added, "The same firm where her husband works."

Mari shot him a dirty look before replying, "My ex-husband. And yes, he works there, which is why I've left."

"I'm sorry," Jesse said kindly while searching inside to see if there was any sense of gladness for knowing this woman from his past was now free. She'd haunted his dreams for years and he knew that his infatuation for her had stopped him from forming any lasting relationships.

Nope, didn't seem to be anything lifting his spirits. In fact, the only thing he felt was a sense of doom. Mostly, he kept catching himself looking toward the kitchen and waiting for Belle to reappear.

Finally, he couldn't stand it. "If you'll excuse me, I'll go and see how Belle's making out with dinner. Just help yourself to more wine."

Mari started to say something and Harry caught her arm to get her attention. While he questioned her about some inane thing to do with their luggage, Jesse escaped.

In the dining area, he found Layla helping her mom put out the silverware and napkins while the pots on the stove boiled away. The smell of the cloves poking from the cooked ham dug deep into his senses and a small stirring of hunger clawed its way past his apprehension.

He sauntered closer. "I've come to help, Belle. I'm all yours."

The sound of disgust she made scorned his words and he knew she was furious. And rightly so!

*I should be shot.* "Belle, let me explain."

Her furious face turned his way for only a second before she once again ignored him. "No need. Mari's finally back in your life. The woman you loved for so long. Kim told me how you've kept her on a pedestal since high school."

"That ended years ago."

Belle knew she was over-reacting. She couldn't put a lock on her jealousy and it showed in her stupid behavior. Taking a deep breath, she said, "I think you need some time to sort out your feelings, Jesse. I'll move back to my apartment for tonight."

"No!"

"Yes!"

"I'll move with you."

"No, you won't. Father and Marilyn can move in here with you where it's more comfortable. We'll take Sam with us so he won't be a bother."

"It won't work. There are only two beds." He knew he sounded sulky but what the hell was a guy to do when met with a rock-wall of female resistance.

"Hell, if Mari won't sleep with you, then you can sleep on the couch."

# Chapter 36

Jesse took offense to her last smart-ass remark and Belle knew it as soon as the mean words left her mouth. Hurt feelings and... face it... jealousy had made her speak without any restraints. His shock, followed by anger, made her aware she'd gone too far.

The evening meal, although delicious, was strained and uncomfortable. The only relief came when Layla had let out a rather unladylike burp and Belle automatically followed it with a "What do you say?"

Much to everyone's amusement, the little girl answered in a manner showing annoyance, "I can't wemember," then looked surprised at the sound of trivial laughter her answer produced.

"You say excuse me when you burp."

"Oh. Do I also say that when I fa—?"

"Lay-la!"

"Billy Arnold says that word."

"No doubt Billy Arnold's mother doesn't hear him say it or she'd correct him."

Layla tried to outstare her mom but it didn't work. "Sow-wy Mama."

Belle shook her head, a grin fighting to break loose. Unable to stop herself, she glanced at Jesse and caught the same reaction on his face. They shared a small moment before she remembered and her food drew her attention once again. The meal plodded on.

Harry reached for the dish of perogies and took more onto his plate. "These are delicious, Belle dear. The store-bought ones aren't anywhere near as good."

Jesse who already had his second helping piled on his plate, piped up. "They're my new favorite food."

"Mine is pizza." Yaya grinned across the table and Jesse winked back.

Harry joined in. "I like pizza too." And that got the two pizza lovers sharing which ones they liked the best. If Layla and her grandfather hadn't kept the conversational ball rolling, the evening would've been a complete fiasco.

Even Mari didn't seem to have any of the earlier vivacity until Jesse went along with her reminiscing, and then she sparkled.

For Belle, the time couldn't go by fast enough.

As she picked at each course, she tried to focus on Layla's conversation. Soon even Layla wound down and Belle used it as a reason to excuse herself.

"I've done most of the clean-up, it's just putting the dishes in the dishwasher and I'll leave that part with you Jesse. I've already moved Layla's and my stuff over to the other place and brought Father and Marilyn's luggage here. It's in the front hall."

Harry frowned at her. "You want us to stay here now?"

"It's for the best. That way Marilyn and Jesse can catch up on old times and I can settle Layla down in her own bed."

A sulky expression flooded Yaya's face. "No Mama. I don't wanna go home. And I don't wanna go to bed."

"Too bad, muffin. You can have a bath. I'll read you your favorite "T'was the Night Before Christmas" book. Then lights out. You're tired, and tomorrow is Christmas Eve. It'll be a long day for you." Honesty had to be faced as she heard her own words; it would be a long day for her more so than Yaya.

A sob escaped as Layla started to fuss. "I wanna stay with Jesse and... and Gwampa." Her words were followed by another sob. When she read the stubborn look on Belle's face, she let loose with the wails. "I don't wanna go to bed." The last words were roared in her don't-mess-with-me voice.

Belle, who knew that the nonsense had to be stopped before Yaya got carried away, lifted her out of her chair. "Tomorrow you can play with Grampa. Now it's time for bed. Say good-night to everyone."

Respecting the note in Belle's tone, Layla sniffed, wrapped her arms around her mom's neck, and murmured, "G'night."

*\*\*\**

Jesse looked around at Mari's expression and saw something that annoyed him. "Belle is a wonderful mother. She was right you know. Layla needs to have an early night."

"Oh, I totally agree. It's just that I've never been in close proximity with a child before. I mean, I've been forced to listen to many brats in restaurants and periodically on plane trips. To tell the truth, that type of behavior totally turned me off little kids. Now seeing how special Layla is and the way Belle handles her, I'm realizing there are methods to deal with the little devils."

Jesse answered with a smile in his voice. "No doubt about it. Munchkins are a handful. When they dig their little claws into your heart, trust me, they can take you to heaven or hell. Either way, you'll find the trip one you'd never want to miss."

After saying his piece, Jesse noticed the look that passed between father and daughter. "Did I say something wrong?"

Harry answered, his face lit up with enjoyment at an inside joke. "Not at all. You said exactly what she needed to hear, didn't he Marilyn?"

She hesitated before nodding and agreeing. "It's a lot to consider. You two go and get acquainted. I'll tidy up here and join you for a nightcap in a little while."

Harry pushed his chair back and caught Jesse's confusion. "Let's leave this young woman alone. She has some very serious thinking to do."

# Chapter 37

Jesse settled Harry with a nightcap and joined him on the couch.

"Can I ask you a question about Belle, Jesse?"

"What do you want to know?"

"She seems a bit under the weather. And I noticed she didn't eat nearly as much as the rest of us. She wouldn't have any perogies or bread, not even some of the apple pie she made for dessert. I'm a bit concerned."

Filtering through how much he could safely tell Harry without crossing boundaries, Jesse took a sip of his drink and put it on the table. "Recently, Belle couldn't keep any food down at all. Then we found out that she has the same symptoms as a person with Celiac disease which means she must have a completely gluten-free diet. You might have noticed that she prepared her food on a different counter. As long as she takes extreme care, her sickness seems to be under control. In the last week, she's gained a lot of energy—and some of her lost weight."

Harry leaned forward and listened carefully to Jesse's explanation. "This Celiac, can it be cured?"

"I don't believe so. Other than having to take added vitamins, watch her nutrition and use common sense, Belle is perfectly fine and can live a normal, healthy life."

Harry smoothed his mustache with shaking fingers. "You seem to know a lot about the ailment."

"I've been reading up on it. The mother of one of my workers' also passed on some information. She's involved in a study at the university and has had Celiac for a number of years." Jesse saw the older man relax, seemingly satisfied that his daughter would be fine.

"Now it's my turn to ask you a question." Jesse watched the other man's reaction and noticed how he stiffened slightly. Jesse added words that might take away his discomfort. After all, Harry was a guest in his home—technically his sister's home, but since he was in charge, it was up to him to play host. "If I'm prying, you can tell me it's none of my business."

"Shoot! If I can answer, I will."

"What's up with Mari and her husband? One minute, the lady's giving me the come-on like we're kids again, and the next minute, she's radiating so much pain that she looks like she'll explode. She says they're divorced. You say no?"

Harry spoke, scorn obvious in his tone. "They're separated and the divorce will be final on the 28th."

"Did she leave him?"

"Yes." Harry hesitated and then continued. "Considering my daughter is a top litigator, she can be quite dense when it comes to men."

"Why? What happened?"

While Jesse watched, Harry sorted through his conscience, deciding what he could say without breaking any confidences. Jesse respected that and didn't push. Finally, after smoothing his mustache a number of times, Harry checked the kitchen door and then spoke in a low voice. "Steve wanted children."

Jesse waited for more but it wasn't forthcoming. "And..."

"And Marilyn didn't."

"So...?"

"He pushed too hard and she left."

The kitchen door closed making the two men jump. "What are you two hatching?" Mari's playfulness sounded as fake as a bad actress in a third-rate movie.

"Nothing, dear." Harry put his empty glass on the table, stood then stretched. "If you show me where my things are and the room you want me to use, I'll be saying good night."

In a no time, Jesse sorted him out and returned to the living room to find Mari had lowered the lights and filled their glasses. Soft music now played in the background. The setting perfectly arranged for seduction.

"Come and sit, Jesse. I've been looking forward to getting you alone so we can catch up on old times."

Apprehensive, like a man would feel if told he had to stick his hand in a snake-pit full of venomous critters, Jesse picked up his glass and went to move to the chair.

"No, here, beside me. I need to talk with you."

Stubbornly, he sat in the chair and leaned toward her. "I can hear very well from here."

If Mari only knew that all he wanted was to go to Belle's place, she might not look so pleased for his company.

In his imagination, he fantasized about how he'd force his way inside and beg Belle to listen to him. Just thinking about the conflict made his stomach tighten. Maybe he'd just whimper like Sam did when he wanted her to pick him up and she'd take pity on him. His nonsense made him smile and Mari, misunderstanding, smiled back with delight.

"It's nice being together again, isn't it, Jess?"

Her calling him by the shortened version of his name instantly transported him to a past where pain and sorrow had been his two best friends. "I missed you when you left, Mari. For a long time, I missed you."

Getting comfy, she leaned back and tucked her legs under her. "I missed you too."

She spoke softly but they were just words, no depth, no passion, only empty words. Maybe she'd missed him to begin with, but she'd moved on. Found a career. Got married.

While he'd hung on to their early romance like a lovesick fool, willing to let the world go by so he could exist in his ridiculous dreams, she'd lost no time in finding a man to take his place.

Shaking away the remorse, knowing he'd spent enough hours and emotion on a love affair that only existed in his head, he decided to be blunt. End this farce of her pretense. She didn't care about him. Oh maybe as an old friend, maybe she even kept sweet memories tucked away of their young love, but now she belonged to someone else.

"Tell me about your husband."

Mari stiffened, uncrossed her legs, and leaned forward. First running her finger around the rim of the glass, she finally took a sip. She took another and then cupped the glass and looked at its contents as if it held the mysteries of the universe. With her head still down, she finally answered, "You mean ex-husband."

"Don't quibble."

She laughed and tried teasing, her gaze taunting him, willing him to play along. "I'd forgotten your habit of sweeping away the bullshit. Cutting to the chase."

"And I'd forgotten your habit of using bad language for shock tactics."

Giggling, she sipped again and rested back against the couch. "You'd like Steve. He has many of your qualities. He's possessive and funny and very smart."

"Hmmm, sounds like the kind of guy you don't easily throw away."

"It wasn't... easy." Mari mocked the last word. "We want different things. I care about him, so I decided to let him go so he could find someone who can give him what he wants."

"How altruistic of you. Break a guy's heart and tell him you're doing it for his own good." Jesse shook his head. "You women are something else. Ever think that maybe Steve has a right to make his own decisions?"

"He made it." She lowered her voice and continued. "We were fighting and I'd frustrated him but he'd reached an impasse I couldn't handle." Her voice rose again, full of anger and anguish and shock. "In fact, he gave me an ultimatum. Have his baby or leave."

"Huh? Thought you told me he was smart?"

"Not so much."

"You gonna give in?" Horrified, Jesse watched Mari's chin begin to quiver.

"I wasn't planning on it until today. Now that I've spent time with Belle and Layla, I'm kind of... ahhh, messed up." Her sobs started out quite low. As soon as he slid onto the couch and gathered her into his arms, she broke.

"You love him, Mari. So give the guy a break. Have his baby and be happy." He sheltered her with his chest and used his hand to pat her back comfortingly.

She struggled to answer and her woeful words made him hate himself for being so blasé about the matter.

"I just... can't."

Thinking fast, he wondered if maybe she had a medical problem. "You mean you can't or you won't?"

"You'll laugh if I tell you."

"Scout's honor, I won't even grin."

"I – I'm scared."

"Of... of the pain?"

"Of course not!" Her disgust at his absurd questioning overshadowed her crying for a few minutes. She sniffed and continued. "I'm afraid I'll be a horrible mother. What do I know about babies? Or kids for that matter? I'm a lawyer. I like to fight battles in a courtroom. I've never even been in a nursery, or for that matter, held a baby."

"Have you told him about your fears?"

"I couldn't. He'd think me a fool and I couldn't bear that."

Her crying had slowed to sniffles and his back pats had changed to rubs. Her head, buried against his chest, making it impossible for him to see her face. Jesse could only guess by the sound of her voice how difficult it would be for her to confess about fearing anything.

After all, as youngsters, she'd been the one thrilled over any reckless kind of activity. He'd always held back from pure common sense but her 'hell-bent for adventure' attitude had often made his eyes cross and his heart end up in his throat.

He used that image now to his advantage. "Marilyn Krude? Frightened of something? That's not the girl I remember. She'd conquer anything." He teased gently, hoping to make her feel better.

"All show. I was always afraid, Jess, but I knew if I screwed up you'd take care of me. Now being in charge of a little person? That's a whole different scenario. I'd be completely out of my element."

"Surely you know someone who's gone through this already, other women with children."

"I've never had many women friends. The ones I do know are strictly career oriented. When we married, I thought Steve wanted the same kind of life I did. Good jobs, lots of travel, nice homes. You know, an exclusive, just the two of us, kind of existence. Then he upsets our safe world by deciding time was moving on and we needed to start a family."

Jesse sat up and made her face him. He wiped her wet cheeks with gentle hands. "Mari, you are a very smart lady. If having a baby is frightening, then learn about it so it doesn't seem so terribly hard. Luckily, you have the perfect teacher as a little sister and she's got a heart as big as Mt. Rushmore. You ask her whatever you need to know. Hell, by the time you've spent the day with her and Layla, you'll want to have a whole brood."

A small giggle broke loose and Mari looked much less upset. "Do you really think so, Jesse?"

"Yeah, I really think so." He reached over and pushed her loose hair back over her ears from where it covered her face. Then he smiled with conviction so she could see how seriously he had taken her predicament.

"Thank you, Jesse. You're a sweet man. In a way, I'm sorry things didn't work out for us." She leaned in to kiss him and he made sure her lips found his cheek. There was no way he wanted to lock lips with a woman who belonged to another man.

# Chapter 38

Belle tossed and turned in her lonely bed. Common sense worked hard to wipe out the emotional response she'd suffered from Jesse's ecstatic reaction at his first sight of Mari. Hurt and bewildered, her mind skipped from one unsettling notion to another.

According to Kim, even though Jesse hadn't seen Marilyn for many years, he'd kept her enshrined in his memories. Even had her framed photograph on his bedside table. Belle had seen the picture turned upside down when she'd dusted the apartment earlier. To keep the memento, he still must have had some attachment to her.

Right?

Maybe not... after all the passion he and Belle had recently experienced, the man showed every sign of being as much invested in their relationship as she was. He'd been a wonderful lover. How could she forget?

What if she'd been too hasty? Perhaps Jesse hadn't meant anything earlier when he'd said Mari's name with such delight? Could be Belle was confusing affection with shock.

Therefore, it made sense that he would react, didn't it? In fact, it would be impossible not to be affected when faced with someone important from your past. Heart truly lightened, she felt better after giving herself the much-needed pep talk.

Resolve firmly in place, Belle slipped out of bed, threw a warm robe on over her pajamas, and checked on Yaya. Sam looked up from the foot of the bed and whined until she went over to soothe his golden velvety skin with pats and comforting whispers. "Good boy, Sam. Good dog."

Then she covered her baby and tiptoed from the room. A side trip to the mirror to brush her hair and apply a bit of lipstick showed her a woman with pink cheeks, a sparkle in her eye, and nerves tightly under control. Ready to apologize, she made her way out of her apartment and quickly down the dim-lit area of the public hallway.

In her mind, she imagined being able to sneak into the foyer area and if everyone were still up, hopefully, she'd be able to catch Jesse's attention. Then she'd give him the signal that she waited for him and zip back home to ready herself for another incredible night.

When she opened the door and stepped into the darkness, she noticed that the bags she'd put there earlier had been cleared. Next, she heard the sounds of soft music. Instantly filled with foreboding, she stepped to the corner and stood rooted to the floor as if imaginary double-sided tape kept her a prisoner.

Not nearly quick enough, she slammed her eyes closed, needing desperately to shut out the image of Jesse leaning back against the couch holding Marilyn in his arms.

While her head rested against his chest, her blonde hair, now loose and flowing, hid her face. His hands rubbed her back in a familiar way of a man soothing a woman he loved.

In the short glance Belle got of his face, Jesse's soft expression exposed such tenderness that it felt like she'd been shot through the heart with a bullet of pain.

Hide.

Run.

Get the hell away.

Oh, the agony! It grabbed, tightening around her chest until breathing became a conscious act. Her hands covered her mouth to keep in the moans. They pressed so hard; she felt the imprint of each tooth against the skin.

She stumbled back against the wall and caught an ornamental angel before it hit the ground. Then she snuck out of the apartment and dragged her broken spirit along with her as she returned to her lonely bed to weep the night away.

# Chapter 39

It seemed to take forever for Marilyn to finally wind down and leave Jesse to make up his bed on the couch. Until his constant yawns did the trick, he thought she'd never leave.

Before he changed his mind, he opened his laptop and did a search on Steve Dangerfield. LinkedIn, the business network with message capability, solved his problem and he sent a personal note to the man who needed a good swift kick in his ass.

Didn't the idiot know that his wife wasn't the kind of a woman who would accept ultimatums and simply agree? The stupid ass should've dug a little and found out why she refused to do something that most women accepted as their role. But then again, men could be really dense when it came to their lovers and wives.

Look at him! He had no room to talk. Right now, he was making up a bed on a couch instead of being wrapped in the arms of the girl who'd become his whole world.

Again, he headed for the entrance only to pull himself up short. You can't just go there and pound on the door at this time of the night. You'll scare Layla or the neighbors. They'll call the police and you'll end up in the drunk-tank.

Despite his yearning to be with her, he paced the room to strategize. How could he get Belle alone so he could explain?

Explain what? That the shock of seeing his past had momentarily rattled his brains. It was the truth. He just had to make her believe it.

As soon as he spotted the two Persian pests who'd been kicked out of Kim's room and were now curling themselves on his narrow couch, he flung himself in the only chair he could comfortably sit in and fumed.

After another glass of wine and an hour of contemplation, exhaustion kicked in. First, he threw an afghan over the chair he'd just left and picked up Puff to transfer her to the new bed. She mewed softly and licked his hand, and with a few strokes settled down quietly.

When he went to move Snowball he was met with a hiss and a glare of resistance. "Not tonight you monster, I'm in no mood." Ignoring the warning, he lifted the cat, moved her next to her sister, and sucked at the claw mark on his knuckle that he got for his troubles. "Damn cat!"

Quickly, he undressed and tried getting comfortable on a bed too narrow, too small, and too empty. Stuffed up from the fur, he rubbed his nose and decided he'd rather have ten Sams than one feline-like Snowball.

Sam!

Why didn't he think of that before? Early in the morning, he'd go and pick Sam up for his constitutional and save Belle from the trouble of having to take the pup out herself.

It would give him the perfect opportunity to explain everything to her, plead if need be. Hell if nothing else worked, he was prepared to grovel.

# Chapter 40

Rising early, after a sleepless night, Belle knew she needed to get away. Spending time with the others couldn't be borne until she'd built up her defenses.

Once Layla woke and Sam began his ritual fidgeting for his morning walk, she still had no plan. When the doorbell rang, her heart dropped like the proverbial stone. She just knew it would be Jesse to get the dog.

"Layla take Sam to the door for Jesse while Mommy's in the bathroom please."

"Okay!"

Belle heard Jesse's deep tones and then her little girl's giggles but she remained hidden until Yaya came to get her. "Jesse wanted to talk with you, Mommy."

"He did?"

"Yep. He said so, but Sam had to go outside real bad."

"Did he say anything else?"

"He said to tell you that he'll keep Sam at his place so we gotta go over there when we're ready."

Belle ruffled Yaya's hair. "It won't be until later. This morning you and I have to go shopping. We still haven't any presents under the tree for Grampa and Auntie Marilyn and tomorrow's Christmas."

"And for Jesse too."

"Yes, we'll buy some little thing for Jesse."

"But weally nice, right Mommy?"

The doorbell rang again and Belle suffered the same reaction as earlier.

*My god, I can't live like this for long. I have to either get a backbone or I'll be a basket case by the end of the week.*

Since Yaya was now getting dressed, Layla had no choice but to open it herself.

Praying it wasn't either Marilyn or Jesse, she checked the peephole and breathed a huge sigh of relief before opening the door to the end of the chain.

"Jack! What are you doing here?"

"I wanted to deliver my Christmas presents for you and Layla. I hope you don't mind."

His calm persona added to what Jesse had told her about Phil's assessment, worked to loosen her fear. Still slightly apprehensive, she unlocked the door and opened it. Then she blocked the doorway and really looked at him.

He'd dressed in civilian clothes and they made her remember Jack as he'd been before he and Terry had joined up. Even his short hair in the wind-blown style of so many of the young men today worked to remove the memory of the wild man who'd accosted her.

Trying to picture this Jack as the animal who'd stolen her baby didn't work either. Not now. Not seeing him looking so well.

He'd lost the begging eyes and sickly aura. Standing tall, his cane by his side, he waited for her to speak. This guy resembled the old Jack, the one she'd missed so badly when he'd changed.

Speaking softly, she asked, "How are you really, Jack?" On the one hand, Belle wasn't sure if she should have anything to do with the man responsible for frightening her to death not that long ago.

Confidence flooded once she spied the two beautifully wrapped presents and the peaceful expression when he smiled tentatively. She opened the door wider. "Come in."

"Thank you, Belle. I hope I'm not too early. I like the mornings and decided to try and catch you before you went out for the day."

"Good thing. We're planning to go shopping for

some last-minute Christmas presents. The stores will be hectic so I wanted to go early. You... you look wonderful, Jack."

"I feel the same way. Jesse hooked me up with a friend of his, Phil Reid, who runs a special program for us Vets. It's been inspirational and a lifesaver. I have a long way to go but it's a beginning."

"Oh, Jack! I'm glad. I was so worried about you."

"I didn't feel too good about myself, either. I can't tell you how sorry I am for frightening you the way I did. Desperation can drive a man to do crazy things. I just hope you know that I'd never hurt Layla. Having her nearby gave me a peace that's hard to explain and it was something I craved."

"You look fine now, Jack. That's why I opened the door."

"It's true. I'm taking a different medication that doesn't make me feel like I'm locked in a nightmare. It's helped tremendously. Plus the group therapy has taught me that the peace is coming from learning how to deal with my fears and not feeling so alone."

Belle reached out to hold his hand. "I'm grateful everything worked out and thankful that you're so much better."

"Phil offered me a position, working beside him and I'm going to take it. Don't worry about me anymore. From now on I want to be able to help you girls." He squeezed her hand before he dropped it and then passed over the presents. "Enough about me." Jack scanned her in a friendly way. "Goodness, you look a lot better than the last few months." When he caught her eye and she looked away, his hand reached but stopped before touching her shoulder. "Something's not right."

"I'm fine, didn't sleep much and it's catching up. My health is a lot better since I found out what my problems were and have corrected them. I won't go into it now, but one day, I'll tell you all about it."

"Uncle Jack!" Layla ran into the room and slowed before reaching the tall man who looked so much like the picture of her daddy.

He knelt down and waited for her to approach. "Hey sweetheart, I came to bring you a Christmas present because I heard on the grapevine that you'd been a very good girl this year."

"I've been the best girl. Mommy and I are going shopping for more pwesents. You wanna come?"

Belle stiffened and so did Jack. His eyes flew to her and he waited. She knew he was silently asking for permission and his consideration charmed her into giving an affirmative nod. "You can help me keep this monster munchkin under control."

# Chapter 41

Jesse came around the corner just in time to see Jack Foster helping Belle and Layla onto the downtown bus. Flashes of anger consumed him and that made him feel guilty. They looked so happy together which was a good thing.

Sam wanted to run to them and he restrained the anxious puppy. Once they'd disappeared, the thwarted dog ran in circles and whined his disappointment until Jesse hauled him to his side and bent to pet the shivering animal. "Hey, pal. I know exactly how you feel."

Jesse picked the pup up in his arms and slowed his pace in comparison as to how quickly he'd moved earlier. Anxious to see Belle, he'd cut the usual routine by quite a bit.

Sam's searching tongue persuaded Jesse to move the nuisance under his arm. Another bus caught his eye and he thought about Belle and the man she'd chosen to spend her time with. He couldn't believe she'd just taken off with Jack who'd frightened the hell out of her only days before.

A thought popped in and made a lot of sense. Maybe she left a message with her sister or her dad. He hurried back inside and met with looks of confusion and dismay.

Harry spoke first and grumbled his distress. "Bloody hell! I wanted to spend the day with Layla and Belle. Why would she leave like that and not include us in her plans?"

Marilyn, who also looked concerned by their absence, wondered aloud, "She might have had chores to do, maybe Christmas shopping that needed to be done on her own, Dad."

"She didn't go alone. Her brother-in-law Jack went with them." Jesse's tone caught both Marilyn and Harry's attention and he knew he had to control his resentment. He didn't own the girl, but after what they'd recently shared, he felt as if she owed him a little more courtesy than to just up and leave with no warning.

Another thing, going out with a man who she'd spurned not that long ago, one who'd ripped her safe world apart, didn't seem too sensible either.

From Phil's last update, he was aware that Jack had come a long way. His medications had been altered and were now working well. It brought some relief, but the worry tearing him apart wouldn't go away. What if she became attracted to her husband's twin? Jesse had sensed the innate goodness in Jack, and Belle already admitted that she'd liked the man in the past.

"Call her and ask her when she'll be home." Harry's insistence brought Jesse's attention back to the others.

"I won't, but you can."

"Okay, I will. I only have a short time with them and I'll be damned if I'll sit around here while they spend the day without me. I'll see if we can meet them somewhere."

While the other two waited, Harry pulled the cell from his pocket and pressed the automatic dial. He let a number of rings pass before slamming it shut. "She's not answering."

# Chapter 42

Knowing that time had run out and she had no more excuses, Belle sighed and put away the wrapping paper and ribbons. Layla, who'd lost interest in the detailed wrap job minutes ago, waited impatiently.

"We're going, honey. You can stop pestering. Grab the small parcel for Auntie and I'll bring the others."

Layla picked up the parcel and then set it down again. Her little face scrunched up as if she were in pain. Belle stopped dead, sensing that whatever was coming would be monumentally important—at least to Yaya. Dressed in a ruffled red blouse and older-girl blue jeans, she looked like a model in a children's catalog. Blonde tufts stuck out over her forehead, and since Belle had taken the time to cut her hair to match the pixie style, it gave her the look of an adorable miniature teenager.

From the frown on her face, Belle sensed that the little miss was troubled. When words finally poured out, they shook Belle to her core.

In a quivering voice, Yaya said, "Mommy, why are you mad at Jesse? Don't you like him anymore?"

Belle sunk to her knees next to the anxious child. "Of course I like him."

"Was he naughty?"

Belle flinched. Goes to show you how much children pick up on the tensions between adults. And here she thought she'd done such a good job hiding her anger in front of the child. Before she could answer, the first drops gathered in Yaya's eyes and then it was like watching miniature waterfalls pouring down both cheeks. Her little baby didn't make a sound. Seems her suffering struck the deepest places in her tiny body and was just too much for her to contain any longer.

Belle felt all twisted up inside. She would have given anything to just lie down on the carpet, cushion her rigid face in her arms and let her own tears loose. Couldn't happen! Not when her child stood in front of her, sobs now racking her body. They quickly turned to open-mouth wails of hurt and misunderstanding. How could Belle expect Yaya to understand? Hell, she didn't have any answers for herself.

Gathering the shaking body close and feeling the tiny arms clutch her shoulders, she hushed Yaya as best she could. "Don't cry, baby. Mommy's not mad at Jesse anymore." Hot, wetness seeped from Layla's cheeks to her neck and felt like acid burning into her skin. Guilt rode her hard. She rocked back and forth while patting the tiny body and making hushing noises.

Finally, the sobs stopped long enough for Layla to catch her breath. "Cou-ouldn't you just give him a time out, Mama? Then he'll be good."

"Why baby, that's a wonderful idea. I'll do that."

"He's pwobably sowwy for being naughty."

"I'm sure he is. Jesse's a nice man."

"He's a vewy nice man. I love Jesse."

"He's enormously lucky then. I have no doubt he missed you today. We'd better rush over there and say hello. Are you feeling better now?"

"Uh-huh!" Layla wiped her chubby hands over her face, smearing the mess of her breakdown from one end to the other. Belle retrieved the tissue she always carried in her pocket for just these emergencies and wiped Yaya's face. Then she held the Kleenex while Yaya blew her nose. "There, all better! You look pretty again."

Yaya gave her a wobbly grin and Belle smiled in return. Overcome with floods of maternal love, she snatched the baby back into her arms, hugged, and stole kisses until riotous giggles reinforced that Yaya was indeed better.

Eventually, they stopped their playful behavior and stood upright. Retrieving the parcels, Belle turned on the lamp and went to close the drapes. Since the late afternoon had darkened the room, she wanted to ready it for their return later.

Shocked, Belle saw the large white flakes and stood spellbound. "Yaya. Come and see. It's snowing outside, baby. Isn't it beautiful?"

Yaya ran to the large window and stood beside her. "Oh, Mommy!" Spellbound, filled with childish delight, she said, "Can we go out to play in the snow?"

"Maybe later, after dinner. We'll see if Grampa wants to go for a walk with us and we'll take Sam on an outing. Now, we'd better go next door."

Remorse ate away at her confidence. Aware that she'd dropped the ball with her family, her conscience had niggled at her all day. Just because she didn't want to be near Jesse, didn't mean that she could mistreat her sister and father. If the many phone calls she ignored were a ruler to go by, they were very annoyed. And with good reason.

When she opened the outer door to Kim's apartment and called out, three voices rang from the inner room.

Her father arrived to confront her first. "About

time! I was ready to call the police and report you two as missing."

Marilyn approached and seemed almost shy. "I'm sorry we couldn't spend the day together. Did you go shopping?"

Jesse held back, and it wasn't until they'd all entered the living room that she saw his displeasure.

Of course, Yaya, thinking Jesse was out of the doghouse, ran to him with her arms raised. When he lifted her and gave her a huge hug, she hugged back with enthusiasm and kisses.

"I missed you, Jesse. Mommy and I went shopping for pwesents and Uncle Jack came with us. He's nice again. But I didn't want to be so long—"

Belle cut in. "Layla. Stop and take a breath. I'm sorry Marilyn, Father. I never meant to be away so long. I wanted to get gifts for everyone and it was crazy-busy downtown. We had to wait in long lines everywhere, and the buses were loaded coming home."

Jesse interrupted. "You could have called and I would have come to pick you up."

She sent him a fake smile. "I didn't want to bother you." Then she turned to the others. "What did you all do today?"

Harry answered with a droll tone that, from what she'd remembered, meant trouble later. "Called you!

Waited for you to get home. We really wanted to spend this time with you and Layla. Now the day is almost gone." Crabbiness rang through loud and clear and intensified her shame.

Marilyn stepped toward Belle as if shielding her from the men's wrath. "It's Christmas Eve, everyone. Let's not waste another minute. What were you planning for the evening meal, Belle?"

"I'll help you get it ready." Jesse's tone brooked no opposition.

No way would she be stuck in the kitchen with him. Especially after Layla had done such a good job on her, softening her resolve to have nothing more to do with the playboy. "I'd rather have Marilyn's help. We haven't had much of a chance to catch up yet."

This time her eagle-eye dared him to argue, and though she knew he wanted to, Jesse backed down. "Call if you need help. Harry and I will play checkers with this whiz kid who laughs at me every time she wins." He lowered Layla who now anxiously exhibited her need to be put down.

"Goodie!" Layla ran to the end table that housed her favorite game.

Belle followed Marilyn to the kitchen and was ashamed when a nasty notion popped into her head. Does she always have to dress in high heels and outfits more suitable for fancy restaurants?

Squashing down the green-eyed monster, she tried even harder to be nice. After all, just because Marilyn preferred dresses to Belle's own choice of well-fitting jeans, whether she liked it or not, Marilyn was part of her family.

A random thought entered and whipped her stomach into an absolute whirlwind. Pray God that doesn't mean that one day I'll be related to Jesse through marriage.

Intruding on her personal nightmare, Marilyn began, "How did Layla handle all the crowds today?"

Good, a subject she loved to discuss. Relief made her relax and she poured a glass of wine for them both. Surreptitiously, she watched her sister whose irrational nervousness made her uneasy. Did Jesse tell Marilyn about their affair? No, he wouldn't. She just knew he wasn't the type of a man to play and tell.

Therefore, Marilyn's behavior didn't make any sense. Shaking off her unease, Belle took out the potatoes and passed Marilyn a peeler while she used the paring knife.

"You know, it's weird. Ever since the other day—"

"It's okay, Jesse told us the story of her going missing."

Belle nodded and continued. "The munchkin

seemed to sense my worry. Today, both she and Jack stayed real close."

Belle went on to describe their trip downtown and began to actually enjoy being with Marilyn, who seemed to have a lot of questions. In fact, they put Belle at ease. Happily, she began to share the best and worst parts of being a mom.

Then Jesse appeared and all the lovely tranquility disappeared. "Can I help you girls?"

Marilyn joked, "Who're you calling girls? Don't you recognize grown women when you see them?"

Belle felt Jesse's glance sear her skin as he answered, his voice husky, "Sorry, my mistake." He reached for her hand as if he had all the right in the world and she pulled away like a fire had scorched her raw. His surprise turned to a frown and then morphed into anger.

But what right did he have to be angry? She hadn't spent the night with another man. Just a day in a crowd with her little girl as her chaperone!

# Chapter 43

That night, dinner again dragged as Belle tried to ignore Jesse's pointed stares. Keeping in mind that Yaya was probably watching them, she was careful to smile and be polite even though it almost choked her. Whenever he spoke, she got up to fix something so she wouldn't have to interact too much.

When he directed a question toward her, she'd mumbled any answer that came to her and promptly changed the subject. Finally, to get him off her back, since it seemed he'd taken to riding her just to be annoying, she turned to Harry and started a conversation between them.

"I'm sorry you're angry about today, Harry. Layla and I didn't mean to stay away as long as we did."

"I get the feeling that being away meant you didn't have to share my company. Baby, I'm sorry I was such a rotten dad, but I'd really like a chance to make up for that by being a much better grandfather."

Belle's heart dropped from the weight of her

shame. She hadn't thought about how her going missing would affect her father. She took his clenched hand in hers, threaded their fingers like she used to as a little girl, and hung on tight. Her eyes begged him to understand as she opened her heart. "Dad, I promise, my staying away today had nothing to do with you. I really didn't mean to be gone so long. Truly, I'm very sorry we didn't invite you to come along."

Harry's eyes glistened and he had to clench his jaw to stop the telltale quivering. "Let me tell you, I was heartsick thinking I'd forced my way in where I wasn't wanted."

"Don't ever talk that way, Dad. I do want you and Yaya's thrilled to have a… a gwampa."

He threw a wobbly smile her way. "She's a miracle. Says we have to go out after dinner and take that crazy mutt for a walk. Guess the snow is calling to her."

"Truth to tell—me too. I love walking in the snow. So, let's worry about cleaning up the kitchen later and get ready now."

Before Belle could make it clear to him that she'd like to keep the trip between her, Layla, and her father, Harry clinked his glass with his spoon to get everyone's attention.

"We're off for a walk in the snow. Anyone else

want to join us, besides Sam?"

Belle wasn't surprised when a short time later they were all wrapped up in mittens, scarves, and warm jackets trudging along on the residential street through the growing banks of snow.

Even Marilyn had changed into slacks and had accepted Belle's ski jacket to wear in place of her expensive coat. She seemed to get into the spirit and acted very happy when Yaya had taken her hand so they could walk together.

Flakes as large as quarters fell from the sky in a never-ending cascade of white and silver, enough to delight both the child and the puppy. And truth to tell, it thrilled the adults too who soon began to act like children themselves.

At one point, Marilyn, looking particularly young and beautiful, decided to show Layla how to make snow angels. While the rest of the adults stood watching them and laughing, the two dropped to the ground where the snow lay pristine.

Jesse, being such a boy, threw snow on them and slipped when he tried to get away. Arms flailing, he landed beside them. Marilyn rolled over him, shouting, "Stop being a pest." Handfuls of snow landed on his laughing face. "We're being angels and you're being a little devil."

Layla, loving the fun, crawled close to his face to

give him instructions on how to be an angel too. "Jesse, just put your arms out and wave them. Up and down."

Jesse grabbed her and cuddling her close, he sat up, threatening her with a cold nose rub. Loving the play, Sam leapt into the fray and tried to lick all three faces at once.

Standing nearby, arms entwined with her father's, Belle watched their fun with envy and sorrow battling against her good nature. Lost in thought, she didn't notice that Jesse had snuck toward her. Reaching up he had her in his arms, lying over his knees while the other two were busy again making their angels.

In a voice filled with laughter, he whispered, "You don't have to make like an angel. It's just who you are." Before she could stop him, he rubbed his cold nose against hers and then hugged her close.

Tears flooded and had to be choked back. Her body couldn't seem to stop from convulsing and, not being a complete idiot, Jesse soon picked up on her distress.

She felt him pull back so he could see what was wrong. His expression scrambled her brains and she didn't know what to think. Protecting her heart, she looked away and refused to look back. He muttered; his voice rough with resolve, "Okay, that does it.

We need to talk." He held her head so that she was forced to return his stare.

She swiped at her cheeks. "Not now. I couldn't bear it."

"Tonight. After the rest are in bed. We'll sneak away and talk, Belle. Promise?"

"Okay. Yes." Belle wrenched away from his arms and rolled over so she could get to her feet. He wanted to talk, did he? What could he say? That he wanted another woman? Sweet Jesus, she already knew.

# Chapter 44

On their way back to the apartment, Layla, firmly riding Jesse's shoulders like a princess who accepted her just dues, was in her element.

Happy for her baby, Belle refused to think about what had just happened in the snow. The mixed signals she'd gotten from Jesse threw her into a tailspin and she didn't know if she could deal with any more emotion without a breakdown.

Feeling physically better didn't mean her mental state had recovered completely. The strength of will she'd relied on to get her to where she was today had deserted her since her illness and it hadn't quite recovered. Now, she wobbled between right and wrong. It was right that Jesse find his happiness. But it was also right that she find hers. Too bad it wasn't something they could do together.

Back at the apartment, they all pitched in and had the kitchen cleared in no time at all. Marilyn produced the fancy box of chocolates she'd brought with her to be added to the Christmas goodies.

Meanwhile, Belle helped Yaya decorate a tray with the cookies they'd baked together. Next, they displayed the works on the coffee table in the living room.

Harry decided he made the best hot chocolate and that they all needed to taste his creation. So a tray of Christmas mugs appeared and were soon passed out, marshmallows decorating each drink.

Jesse, being hounded, finally agreed to play Christmas music and the glowing tree and twinkle lights threw a wonderful radiance of holiday spirit around the room.

Everyone was in an especially great mood—except for Belle. She worried that her heart, already sore and heavy, had yet to take one more lash of pain when Jesse broke things off between them.

Not that they had anything serious to end. After all, they'd only been together for two nights—albeit two of the most wondrous nights of her life. But then, men didn't feel the same about these kinds of things.

"Jesse, dance with me." Marilyn held out her hand and forced him to take it. Being a gentleman, he had no choice and Belle understood it on one level. On the heart level, all she wanted to do was push Marilyn aside and let her know she was messin' with

Belle's man.

"Sweetheart, wanna dance with your ugly old man?" Returning to the moment, Belle noticed that Jesse had picked up Yaya and had included her in his dance with Marilyn. The pain lessened and she took her dad's hand.

"I'd love to dance with the handsomest man in the room."

They both laughed when Jesse let out a roar of disapproval. "Hey, that hurts!"

No one heard the doorbell at first. Not until the song came to an end and the bell rang continuously, annoyingly.

"Who can that be?" Harry questioned Belle and a tiny fear grew. *Maybe Jack? God no!*

Jesse went to the foyer and stopped. "Stay here until I find out who it is."

Belle heard a man's loud voice overriding Jesse's and she quickly picked up Layla and hid her face against her neck. She backed toward the bedroom and waited, not being able to leave completely until she knew that Jesse wasn't in any danger.

A man stomped into sight, a stranger covered in snow and looking half-frozen. She still had no idea who he was until she heard Marilyn speak up.

"Steve? What in the world are you doing here?"

"I've come for my wife, is what I'm doing here.

You took off and left no address. By the time I figured you'd be with your stepfather and found his name in your files, you'd left there also."

"Why did you follow me?" Marilyn stepped closer, her cheeks bright and her hands shaking.

"To bring you home. I've changed my mind, Mari. I don't care about kids. Without you, kids don't matter."

Marilyn's smile shone with delight. "You're too late."

"Aww, Mari. Don't say that." Steve hesitated.

"I've changed my mind too. I want to have your baby."

Belle looked from the two in the center of the room to the man who stood nearby, hands in his pockets and a grin on his face.

What in the world? His heart must be breaking and he was covering it up. She couldn't stand by and watch him lose his love a second time.

She passed Layla to her father, nodded to the other room, and waited until they left. Then she went to confront the two who seemed like players on a stage. "I don't know why you're here, buddy, but Marilyn has left you. She wants another man now. You have to accept that you've lost her and move on."

Marilyn's stunned expression threw Belle for a

second but didn't deter her from her goal.

Steve swung her way. "A... another man? What the hell are you talking about lady?"

"I'm not a lady, I'm her sister." Belle didn't quite get why Jesse had a grin on his face when she turned to point at him. "He's her real love."

"What?" Jesse stiffened, his yell of rage loud against the sound of Blue Christmas playing in the background.

"Are you crazy?" Marilyn swung from Belle to Jesse and back to Steve. Then she shook her head. "Steve, I swear, he's an old friend. Since we met, there's never been anyone but you."

Steve, lost in the moment, pushed past Belle and never realized she'd move forward at the same time. His body shoved hers and she couldn't get her footing.

Jesse reached her in time to stop her from a bad fall and he scooped her up and moved in front of her. Then he turned to Steve. "Man, you'd better calm down before we have words."

"There's nothing to say, man! I'm taking my wife home and you can't stop me."

***

Jesse couldn't continue to let the fellow scare everyone with his out-of-control behavior, nor could he have Marilyn think any less of the man who obviously loved her. There weren't that many choices and so he took the one he knew would settle the situation with the best outcome of all.

He lifted the smaller-built guy by the front of his shirt so his feet weren't quite touching the floor and he started to walk him to the door.

In a really low voice, he said, "Steve. Punch me."

"Are you crazy?" Steve whispered.

"You want your wife back; you fight for her and make it look convincing."

Steve struggled and Jesse let him go so there would be enough room for the other to take a swing. Still, the man seemed undecided. "Look, I e-mailed you the address. She needs to believe you're for real and that you want her so much you'll do anything. Dammit, hit me."

Who knew the smaller man had such a punch. Jesse saw stars while he massaged his jaw. Then he saw the beloved face of his woman as she raced to his side and cradled him in her arms.

"Hey darlin', it's okay. I'm fine"

Belle knelt beside him with her arms tightly wrapped around his neck, squeezing his sore face, but Jesse knew he'd never said anything more truthful in his life.

# Chapter 45

After Jesse had taken the blow and went down like a man with a glass jaw, all hell had broken loose. It seemed like forever before he had the place to himself and Belle.

Once they'd finally settled the misunderstanding, Steve had grabbed at the offer Jesse made for them to use the other apartment and have it to themselves. Seemed appropriate enough since they had fences to mend and Jesse had a doghouse to get out of.

Before they left, Steve managed sufficient time alone with Jesse to say what had to be said. "Thanks, man. You don't know how much I appreciate your help."

Actually, he did. Not being the time for explanations, he just held out his hand and decided when the other shook it firmly that he liked the man.

Throughout the chaos, one fact struck him that he wouldn't dispute—best he keep Belle close by so she didn't shut down again. If forced to, he'd override any objections she made.

Once she realized his ploy for getting the other two lovebirds alone, she became less difficult. Indeed, she got right into it by being a wonderful hostess and clearing her and Layla's things out so they wouldn't be disturbed in the morning.

Now Jesse's world didn't seem near as gloomy. After Belle rushed to his side to defend him, he stayed close... even while she whizzed around making everyone as comfortable as possible.

Thinking back to Mari who had thrown herself into her husband's arms and wouldn't let go, mistakenly afraid that he might continue to attack him, Jesse grinned. Hell, it took until the poor guy looked over Mari's shoulder and caught Jesse's wink that he started to get with the program. Then he couldn't get Mari alone fast enough, probably to start working on the baby they both now decided was the biggest thing they had to accomplish in the New Year.

Jesse continued his musings while Belle helped Layla and her 'Gwampa' set up a tent in Kim's bedroom by her big window. The delightful imp wanted to watch for Santa. Ten minutes after both babies, canine and human, had crawled onto the makeshift mattress, they'd drifted off to dreamland. Harry was more than happy to take up residence on the nearby bed to stand guard with Snowball and Puff for sleeping partners.

That left Jesse's bedroom free. His goal to woo the woman he loved and talk her into sharing his bed was now in operation.

First, he had something he had to do. He sauntered over to the larger branch on the Christmas tree where he'd left a parcel wrapped all in gold and retrieved it. The present's significance had driven him crazy with doubts since he'd bought the darn thing.

He hoped she'd be happy... no, he prayed she'd be happy to see what he'd bought for her to wear.

# Chapter 46

Belle still didn't understand what had happened earlier. One minute, she was accosting a threatening stranger and the next he'd turned into a bewildered relative.

That he'd punched Jesse and managed to knock him down still didn't register. Jesse was a big man, lean and strong, with muscles everywhere on his body.

Steve, in contrast, looked to have a runner's build, slim, compact, and six inches shorter. Something didn't compute. She couldn't stand it another minute.

"How did Steve come to hit you?"

"Just a lucky punch, I guess." Jesse wouldn't look Belle in the eye and she had a feeling there was a cover-up going on. With his back to her, he walked over to the tree and was searching for something. It gave her a moment to filter through the evening.

One thing she knew for sure, not only did Marilyn

love her husband, but they would be staying together to start a family. And it was because of her and Yaya that Marilyn had overcome her fears about motherhood.

Secretly, it made her swell with pride to think that they'd made such a good impression. Every woman tries her hardest to be a good mom, but many times it wasn't noticed by outsiders. When it is, and commented on, darn but it felt great.

The acknowledgment probably shouldn't matter if one knows they're doing their best, but it did. The lightness floating inside Belle certainly made her happy.

If she were being entirely truthful, it could be that the happiness existed more from realizing that Jesse and Marilyn were not back together. That maybe she'd mistaken what she saw the other night—a sweet interlude between old friends, rather than an intimate moment involving lovers.

Jesse, holding the small golden gift in his hand, the same one he and Yaya bought the other day, approached slowly. Watching his advance cranked up her pulse to where she felt quite dizzy.

The dryness in her mouth forced her to lick her lips and she found quick swallows of the cooled hot chocolate helped, though it didn't do anything for the shakes that developed deep inside her stomach.

They quickly traveled through her entire system until she thought she'd pass out. She managed a few deep breaths before Jesse sat close to her on the sofa, his fragrant after-shave a reminder of other intimate moments.

The enticing magic of the sexual tension, interwoven with her overwhelming love for the man, drove her half-crazy with need.

Shy, scared he'd see the hunger in her eyes, she gazed away from him to where the atmosphere of Christmas surrounded them in its enchantment. From the multi-colored lights and ornaments decorating the tree, which was now loaded with presents underneath, to all of Kim's other holiday treasures, it screamed of the season to be jolly.

Jesse got her attention when he put his arm behind her on the back of the couch and whispered her name.

"Belle. I know there have been difficulties between us these last few days. As a mere man, I can't begin to understand what's going through your mind." He put the gift in her hands and very gently cradled her cheek. "Is it enough that I desperately want to try and understand? Can you tell me what's been worrying you? I'd like everything settled between us before I ask you to open my present."

"Oh, Jesse, I think I've been very foolish. The

truth is, when you first saw Marilyn and reacted the way you did, I'll admit to being jealous. And it took me a while to come to my senses. Eventually, after I figured that it might have been shock that made you react the way you did, I came back to get you. That was around ten last night."

His hand dropped and he stiffened. "At ten? You came here to the apartment?" Jesse's frown said it all.

"Yes."

"Oh honey, I'm so sorry. If you'd spoken, you would have realized I... it looked bad, didn't it?"

"Oh yeah! Real bad."

He nodded and swept his hand through his hair. Then he rubbed his thigh and cleared his throat. She could see when he came to the obvious conclusion. "That's why you changed. Look, I can explain."

"You don't have to."

"Honey, don't be mad. Please trust me—"

"I do."

"You do?" He stared at her as if she had just morphed into an angel.

She couldn't stop a tender smile from appearing. He was an endearing man and she was nuts about him. "I do trust you, Jesse. It didn't come easy. I had to have a good talk with myself. But I came to realize that most probably it was a tender moment between old friends. I'm right, aren't I?"

"She was very unhappy."

"I don't need to know the intimate details."

"I really would like to tell you, Belle, but it's Marilyn's story, not mine."

"I kinda figured that by the way you were holding her. At first, the shock made what I actually saw unclear. I was hurt and angry. Then you gave me that look in the snow and I wondered if I'd made a mistake. Upon re-visiting the scene, I came to understand that there must have been more to the incident than I'd picked up at first glance."

"What look? You mean the one I'm using now?"

She swayed toward him. Her bones weakened. Every nerve ending on her body woke up and became sensitized. "That's the one." The sweet agony of knowing how much she meant to him floated between them soft and gentle. How incredible it was that he wanted her so desperately.

She inched closer and Jesse put his arms around her as if he couldn't stand not being physically linked. Her eyes sought his and the look of pure adoration lifted her heart right out of her chest where it met his and connected.

What woman, who knew herself so cherished, wouldn't yield? He scooped her into his arms and she nestled on his knees. His hungry lips dove in to claim hers and the world faded.

The kiss promised so much.

A man she'd treasure every day while they built a life together.

A wonderful father for Yaya to love and any other children they might have.

And his love that would keep her safe forever.

The sound of the gift dropping onto the floor caught Jesse's attention and he pulled away just enough to retrieve it.

"I need you to open this now and say you'll wear it for me." The throaty way Jesse spoke made her realize that for him this moment was precious.

Trembling, full of joy blended with anxiety, Belle took the parcel and unwrapped the fancy bow. Inside, she found a small red velvet box.

Before opening it, she looked up and caught his eye. Scared that he'd gone a bit faster than she'd expected, she hesitated. Was she ready? Another searing glance and her heart settled into the rhythm of commitment.

She opened it. There on the white satin lay a stunning heart of diamonds with the silver chain threaded through.

"It's so beautiful." She whispered the words because her emotions had overwhelmed her ability to talk out loud.

"I hope you'll agree to wear it, honey. I don't want

to sound corny but it represents my heart that I want to give to you, to keep safe."

"Oh, Jesse. I love it. Help me put it on." She lifted her hair while he gently set it around her neck. "I'll treasure it forever."

He kissed the heart where it lay against her neck, sending shockwaves over her vulnerable skin. "When you're ready, we'll add a diamond ring to match. I didn't want to rush you, but there's an intense need in me to make you mine." He kissed her very softly there again and then worked his way back to her lips.

Needing to clear away the tiny niggling unease that she couldn't shake off no matter how many times she told herself not to worry, Belle pulled back a bit and watched his expression. "Kim did tell me that you'd loved Marilyn for many years. That... that she'd broken your heart. Jesse, you have to be sure."

"Of course I'm sure, Belle."

"But how can you be so positive? She's everything a man could want."

"But she's not you."

# Chapter 47

Belle gazed at the splendor of her wedding finery in the mirror and forced the expected tears back. Since the doctor had given her the wonderful news of her pregnancy, everything made her cry. Silly as it sounded; the happier she was the more emotional she'd become.

When Marilyn accepted her request to be her maid of honor, she bawled like a baby. And when Kim agreed to be the bridesmaid, her tears fell in a continuous stream until her neighbor made a joke and got her laughing.

She couldn't seem to find the turn-off valve. And in the meantime, poor Jesse tried his best to get used to this idiosyncrasy. His wanting to please her, so she'd be herself again, just made her weep more because of his good nature. Once she assured him that she'd been exactly the same way for the first three months of Layla's pregnancy, he'd relaxed. After that, he'd play it cool, give her a hug and skedaddle out of her way.

Hugging herself, thanking the Lord for her good fortune in finding such a wonderful partner, she gazed raptly at her reflection. Taking their duties seriously, Marilyn and Kim had shopped with her to help find the perfect dress. Never would she have picked such a design, but urged by the other two, she conceded that their choice had been the right one.

Elaborate, the beaded lace bodice enhanced her body, and even the thin lace, off the shoulder sleeves that ended as a panel of lace in the back, added to the overall effect of stunning glamour. That the dress hugged her stomach midway and then began a gentle flare meant she'd be comfortable throughout the long evening of festivities. And the tiny human nestled in her tummy wouldn't be constricted in any way.

The door opened and both Marilyn and Kim returned... Kimmy carrying a box of tissues. "I knew you'd need these if we left you alone for five minutes."

Smiling, Belle pulled out one and then a few more to tuck away in the bodice of her gown. "Did you find Layla? She needs to put her dress on now."

"She's with Jesse. I'll go and fetch her." With a pat on Belle's shoulder, Kim left the room. Marilyn came up behind her until both images were visible in the full-length mirror. They smiled at each other and Belle saw Marilyn's hand gently pat the tiny bulge in her own stomach.

"Do you feel a little better now? Did the fresh air help?"

"Actually, yes. I'm glad Kim insisted we go outside for a few minutes. Sorry to leave you alone at a time like this." Marilyn smoothed the chiffon and lace front of her coral gown. She and Kim had chosen to wear the same color, only different styles, and they both looked perfect.

"Not to worry. I had a little cry and feel better for it."

Marilyn laughed. "God, Belle. I'd give up this morning sickness any day and gladly drip tears like you. I don't think you've been sick once, have you?"

"No, but it's kinda embarrassing for the store clerk when he has to deal with a ditzy customer blubbering because he said the peaches were on sale."

"Maybe you're right. Truth to tell, I'm so happy to be pregnant that I'll gladly put up with upchucking every few hours. And Steve is delighted—struts around like he personally invented the sperm cell."

Giggles claimed the women until they both ended up grabbing for the box of tissues.

They turned to the noise at the door. In

scampered Layla with Kim right behind. "Can I put my dwess on now, Mama?" Since she'd taken to choosing her own clothes, Belle never knew how she'd look when she came out of her room in the morning. This day, she'd donned her favorite pair of dungarees and teamed them with a bright purple blouse, a size too small. Belle hoped she could find another top in the same color so she could wean the stubborn little miss from wearing this one.

"Yes, baby. Is Jesse dressed now?"

"Nope! We were playing a card game. But he has his clothes all spread on the bed so he said he'll be weady in two shakes of a dog's tail." Giggling uproariously at her favorite person's witticism, Layla's expression of adoration let everyone know that her Jesse could do no wrong. "And Gwampa is there now and Uncle Steve. They're in their suits and look stunned."

"You mean stunning." Belle smiled and wiped the fresh waterworks from her eyes.

"Okay. Can I put my dwess on *now?*" Her eyes glowed with the thought of finally being able to don the dress she'd stared at every morning for weeks.

"Yes, sweetheart. It's in my closet. I brought it in here so you could be with us to get dressed."

Kim quickly went to the open door and lifted the tiny white gown from the hanger. The draping, coral satin belt contrasted beautifully with the white lace in the miniature replica of her mother's wedding dress.

With both Marilyn and Kim helping, it only took a few minutes to have the child ready. Her natural curls were brushed and shone. "Auntie Mawi, can I have flowers in my haiw like Mommy does?"

The women stopped dead in their tracks. No one had thought she'd make this request. Marilyn piped up and said, "Of course, Yaya. I'll just take a couple of the flowers from your mom's bouquet and we'll pin them on." Working quickly, Marilyn fashioned a gathering of flowers she extracted from the huge bunch that the florists had delivered. She braided a small amount of Layla's hair, tucked the colorful blooms in, and pinned them securely." There, you like?"

"I like." Layla preened at herself and then decided they needed to take a selfie with her new/old phone, a gift from an adoring Jesse who'd gotten an upgrade. After shooting three with varying, silly faces, they could barely speak.

A loud knock stopped their hilarity. Harry stuck his head in. "Am I interrupting you ladies?" His face, wreathed in smiles, tugged at Belle's heartstrings. She quickly bit her lip to stop the coming waterfall. This time it worked and she took a deep breath.

When a girl's every dream had come true, from the beautiful new home that Jesse had built for them, to having everyone in her world who she loved together to celebrate her wedding, the music in her heart seemed reasonable.

Before shepherding the ladies who'd gathered their flowers and formed the proper lineup—Belle on one arm and Layla holding his hand—Harry filled his pockets with tissues. Then he led his entourage to where his soon-to-be son-in-law stood waiting, smiling, his eyes full of tears.

# Afterword:

Thank you so much for reading **She's Not You.**

I loved writing this story and I hope you enjoyed reading it. If so, I would ask you for a favor. Wherever you purchased this book, please take a few minutes and leave an honest review. Authors enjoy hearing that readers like their stories, and hopefully, others will read your words and choose to buy them because of your sentiments.

My website at **http://mimibarbour.com** now has all my books listed with links to the various publishers to make it easy for you to find my other work.

While you're there, I'd really appreciate it if you would sign up for my newsletter so I can keep in touch.

http://bit.ly/mimibarbournewsletter

I only send out newsletters approximately once a month and you have my word that your address will never be shared.

*Hugs, Mimi*

P.S. As a special gift for you, I have included the 1st chapter of the next book in this series *Love Me Tender.*

*Love Me Tender*

*Elvis Series – Book #2*

by
Mimi Barbour
NYT & USAT Bestselling, award-winning
author

A child, a puppy, and sweet romance...

Anne Pichette is an eighteen-year-old exchange student who goes to live in Texas for a year. Rose Walsh, her host mother, treats her like a daughter and Anne believes her life is perfect. Rose's teasing, devilishly handsome son, Clint, on whom Anne develops a crush, has a lot to do with this belief. One night, Anne shares her tender passion with Clint, but sadly, he's too inebriated to remember. A week later, she returns to Paris devastated—and pregnant. Anne fully intends to tell him about her condition except her plans are deterred due to a letter arriving announcing his impending marriage to a pregnant woman he loves. Eight years later, Rose appears in Paris to beg Anne to come back to Texas to help her through her final days of cancer. Unable to refuse her dear old friend, Anne accepts. Now she'll have to divulge that her boy, Max, is Clint's son.

Clint Walsh might be hardened and embittered but he knows he has a good reason for acting this way. After all, his wife, the slutty woman he believed was his true love, leaves him with their daughter and never looks back. So how's a man supposed to handle that kind of treachery? Especially after they'd shared one beautiful night of lovemaking he's never been able to forget. Or, due to his state of intoxication—clearly remember.

Praise:

"The first thing I have to say is that I love heroes who have rough edges that need smoothing... by none other than the heroine, of course. Clint is one of those heroes! He's a rough and tumble cowboy whose heart has hardened. Annie is just the woman to give him what he needs so that he can heal and love again. Right from the beginning, I wanted these two to end up with a happy forever future.

The children in the story, Max and Debbie, add a realism and a very touching aspect to the story. I couldn't help but love them.

This is a wonderful, slightly spicy romance that I thoroughly enjoyed."

~ *Reviewed by D J Faz*

"This is a wonderful sweet story of love. There is

sadness too but love overrides all. Love Max and his strong personality and his love of horses. Debby is as sweet as can be. You can't help but want to just hug those two kids. Loved this book and so recommend any and all of Mimi's books. We all need a little "Mimi time" to brighten our days!

~ *Reviewed by Shirleen*

# Chapter One - Love Me Tender

Anne looked at the clock once again, and relief overtook her uneasiness. Only one more hour for the shop to be opened, and then she could get home to her son, Max. For some unknown reason, she'd felt nervous all day.

Standing at the large window and looking out into the night, Anne saw that the street lamps and other stores put a glow throughout the street that gave a light of safety for the crowds of laughing people. It seemed that everyone had a direction; they were heading somewhere. This thought woke up a sadness that had been growing inside Anne for quite a while. Her life seemed so empty while the rest of the world had a purpose. She had no doubt this distraction had something to do with the fact that she had no partner—no mate—no-one special to make her feel glad to be a woman.

The last fellow she'd broken up with hadn't been

able to hold her attention and that seemed to be an ongoing problem. No man attracted her enough for her to lose herself in him. Was something wrong with her? She'd begun to wonder. Or could it be that one man had made her standards so high that no one else had a chance? Whatever the problem, she yearned to meet a like soul who would sweep her off her feet and fill that aching emptiness inside.

Rubbing her arms to get rid of the shivers flaring up again, she turned from the window and moved to get back to work.

Over the years, she'd learned not to ignore her senses. Not that she was psychic or anything like that. But these *feelings* tended to be warnings that something big would soon rip apart her comfortable world.

To keep the unease at bay, Anne cleaned the table where her last customers had finished their chocolate éclairs and their specialty drinks and left her quite a nice tip for the service. The people of France were known for their love of finer tastes, and nothing satisfied them more than sweet pastry that melted in their mouth.

Normally, Anne wouldn't be here so late, but her evening clerk had called in sick at the last minute, and she couldn't find a replacement. Since she had been at the shop since five that morning, with only a four-hour break in the middle of the day, she was beat. If she wasn't such a stickler for the rules, she'd have shut down early and gone home. But she couldn't. Instead, she took the bucket from the back and started cleaning, so when they re-opened the next morning, much of the clean-up would be done. Besides, keeping busy would make the time go by faster.

She headed for the mirrored, glassed-in cabinets and the counters where silver trays of different chocolates battled for attention with the delicious and decadent truffles, tarts, and candied delicacies that made the store so colorful. The floor near these shelves always ended up with a certain amount of mess made by the clerks handling the trays of goodies.

The bell over the door of *Beaux Rêves* (Sweet Dreams) rang and caught her attention. Her patisserie shop, situated in one of the busier areas in Paris, was always crazy during the day and even into the evening. She wasn't surprised to see more customers at this time.

At first, shadows darkened the face of the woman who entered. Though once she stepped into the light, she looked strangely familiar.

"Hello, Annie."

The sweet timbre of her voice brought instant

recognition.

"Rose!" The mop fell to the floor with a bang. Anne rushed to embrace the woman who had been like a mother to her when she was a young girl of eighteen. Leaving home—her first time away—and living as an exchange student in a small Texas town, and experiencing the strange environment of a ranch had been a struggle. This woman had added joy and given her a year she'd never forgotten. "You didn't write to tell me you were coming. I would have met you at the airport. How very wonderful! Are you here alone?"

Rose burst out laughing. "You certainly haven't changed, hon, other than your accent is strong again. You're still full of questions." She hugged Anne hard. Then she planted kisses on both of Anne's cheeks and one on her nose for good measure. It had been a habit they'd started when Anne had first moved into Rose's house. In those days, she'd been young, scared and rather shy.

Not so much now! Creating her own business from the ground up had hardened her, and becoming a mother had given her a grown-up role that she played very well. "It's lovely to see you." A soft rush engulfed Anne and her cheeks hurt from the large smile stretching her features.

"I wanted to surprise you. Plus, I knew I'd need to

rest after the flight. So I waited to find you until I could handle the excitement. I called the house and your father said you were still at the shop. I gotta admit, my body is all screwy from the overseas flight. Once I woke up, I knew I wouldn't get to sleep again until much later. Considering your place is right in town, I'd strategically arranged a close hotel so I could walk here."

Despite the joy Anne felt at seeing her old friend again, fear also flooded her insides. This was a woman with keen eyes and a very sharp brain. And Anne had a secret.

But she loved Rose more than anyone, other than her own father and her son. "Come and sit down. How silly of me to keep you standing. Rest and I'll organize refreshments."

"Do you have any of those mango tarts you used to make for us on the ranch?"

"You know what? I do. In fact, they're one of my best sellers."

In no time at all, Anne had the table set with her lovely embellished dishes and the sweets organized on a tray. Proud of its interior, and the small touches that made her patisserie so unique, Anne's pride carried over to her vast inventory. Each of the counters and the enclosed glass shelves were arrayed with confections of delight, not only for the eye, but also the stomach.

During the time she worked, she questioned Rose about the trip. But once she sat down at the quaint, glass-topped table across from her old friend, she stopped chattering and got to the point. "How are you, Rose? I know there's something wrong. I can see it in your eyes. You must tell me what's making you so sad."

"I never could hide anything from you, could I?" Anne watched as Rose looked around her. A huge smile of pleasure and an obvious pride lit her features.

"It's just like I imagined from your letters and the numerous pictures you sent over the years. You must be very proud of yourself, kiddo."

Anne felt a lump form in her throat after hearing the special nickname that her surrogate mother had used for the whole year she'd lived with her. "I haven't been called that for so long. It's lovely to have you sitting across from me and calling me kiddo again. I've missed those times." She stretched across and lifted the other woman's hands, squeezing the soft wrinkled, work-worn skin.

Rose returned the pressure and finally looked at Anne, letting the younger woman read her eyes. "I've wanted to be able to say it for so long, but you never came back. And, I couldn't leave the ranch long enough to travel any distance, especially from Texas to Paris."

"But you're here now." Anne saw her old friend's sadness envelope her expression, and if she wasn't mistaken, there was a hint of tears lurking behind her lashes.

"You look wonderful, Annie. So grown-up and chic! You're wearing your hair shoulder-length now, and it suits you." Rose tipped her head to the side. "I like the modern style, and your makeup makes you look so different. If I hadn't recognized your beautiful smile; I might have walked out again, thinking I had the wrong place."

"Thank you." Anne grinned her pleasure. "And Rose, I'd love to return the compliment and say you look good, but we'd both know it to be a lie. Something's wrong, something you're not telling me. Please share, and let me help."

Rose purposely picked up her tart and took a bite in order not to have to answer. And she took her time chewing, motioning that her mouth was full, and she couldn't speak.

"You'll finish it sooner or later, Mama-Rose. And then you'll have nothing to hide behind. I won't let you rest until I know what's wrong." Then a horrible thought attacked and she felt her heart begin to race. "Is it Clint? Has something happened?" Her voice had risen and she hoped the other woman hadn't heard the sheer terror secreted behind her words.

"No, child. No! He's the same. Well, not the same man you would remember. After his wife Cathy left, he turned bitter and hard-hearted. Only his little girl, Debbie, and I can get a smile outta him sometimes, but we have to coax real hard."

"His wife left?" A pole over the head couldn't do more damage to Anne's stability than those words.

"Yes. More'n six years ago, now. I never wrote to you about it because I respected his privacy. We certainly aren't allowed to mention her name in the house, or anywhere that he can hear it. Otherwise, he's miserable for days." Rose sadly shook her head. "Where did it all go so wrong? He thought the sun rose and set on that woman, and all she did was break his heart."

Anne squeezed the hand she still held. "I'm so sorry. You never said anything in your letters. Other than writing about Debbie, and the rest of the gossipy news you knew I loved; you so seldom mentioned Clint. I guess I took it for granted that he was happy."

After hearing these words, Rose stared at her. Like a laser, she penetrated the hard shell Anne had built around her teenage emotions. Hidden for years, the agonizing crush she'd had for a man, who'd treated her like a lost puppy, had laid buried under a steely determination to wipe him out of her head. The young Clint had strutted around the ranch as if God had built the world especially for him to have a playground. He'd been spoiled by everyone who came in contact with him: his parents, the people in the nearby town of Walsh Creek, and, of course, any female he'd deemed worthy of his attention. Clint Walsh had had it all going on, and he knew it.

Rose coughed on purpose, and Anne zeroed back in on their conversation. "Annie-girl, you never mentioned him either. At first, I wondered if you were angry with Clint for something he'd done. I even questioned him about it and you know what?"

Anne stilled. In fact, everything inside her body came to instant attention. "What?"

"It was the first time, in his life, that my boy told me to mind my own business. He didn't talk to me for a long time afterward. So, I learned my lesson. You were off-limits. I often wondered why."

Anne picked up the mugs of cold coffee, intending to go where the huge espresso machine sat on the counter. Before she could step away, Rose grabbed her arm. "See! You aren't as rude as Clint, but you never answered my question either."

"Oh, Rose, please don't fret about me and Clint. It was all a long time ago. Close to nine years have passed, and I truly wished him only happiness. Hearing that he's been hurt is horrible news." This time Anne dropped the veil and let Rose see the sincerity she couldn't hide. Nothing covered the truth when it was heartfelt.

A sob escaped, and Rose lowered her head into her hands. Her shoulders shook with emotion so unfamiliar in the stoic, hard-working ranch wife that Anne used to know. Fear engulfed her, tightening her stomach muscles to a painful intensity. The headache, she'd fought off all day, reappeared with a vengeance. This woman had been the only mother she'd ever known, and Anne loved her dearly. Seeing her in pain was unbearable.

"*Chérie, mon Dieu!* What is it? You're overwrought. You must tell me at once!"

**If you wish to continue reading this lovely story, click here for Amazon – http://myBook.to/ lovemetender

## About the Author:

MIMI BARBOUR: New York Times & USA Today Best-selling romance author has written 5 series and over 35 books. She lives on the beautiful East coast of Vancouver Island and writes her books with tongue-in-cheek and a mad glint in her eye. The fans all agree that it's the fascinating characters she creates which makes her writing so entertaining and brings them back for more of her magic.

"The favorite part of my job is meeting the characters from each new book. Designing them the way I want and having them act however I think they should. It's thrilling, especially when most of my make-believe folks are so very interesting. They're fun and surprising, and in most cases, people I would love to interact with in reality."

# Contact Information:

My website: http://www.mimibarbour.com/

Or my blogspot: http://mimibarbour.blogspot.com

Or follow me on twitter: https://twitter.com/
MimiBarbour

Or on Facebook:  Mimi Barbour Fan page

Or on her Newsletter: http://mimibarbour.com/
contact.html#newsletter